I0537378

FTB Presents:

ODDisms:

An

Anthology

FTB Press, LLC.

Chandler, AZ USA

Printed in the USA.

ISBN-13: 978-0692649763 (FTB Press)

ISBN-10: 069264976X

Table of Contents:

Introduction:

ook Rick Santorum up on Urban Dictionary.com. What you find has less to do with the former Senator and more about what we think of politicians as people. Nothing but the slimy residue left on bed sheets after a wild sexual experience. This is important because the Gods of the Internet can have an entire website dedicated to alternate iterations of regular everyday words and turn them into Pop Culture lingo and have completely dropped the ball on one word—ODDism (as of this printing). This book is an attempt to bring the word into everyday vernacular.

ODDisms is a collection written by a group of talented authors from around the globe who attempt to find meaning in an undefined word. The stories are of strange beliefs and practices which take the characters into oddball situations. Everyone has their quirks, but what happens when the quirks become a philosophy or belief systems? Let's find out.

The staff at FTB Press hopes you enjoy our second anthology. We value the hard work of all the authors and proudly provide a vehicle for them to share their wonderful words with the world. Please enjoy their work in FTB Press Presents: ODDisms: An Anthology.

Cheers!

Scott Lange

FTB Founder

ODDMENT

By

J.J. Steinfeild

You are an odd oddity
an oddment of extraordinary beauty
I hear the busker sing
raspy, rugged, angry at the pedestrians
at the world, other worlds.
I take out a loonie and a toonie
put them back in my pocket
find two quarters in another pocket
one of which I noticed earlier
was minted the year I was born
the other the year of the first moon landing
strange, the things I notice in mid afternoon
toss them in the busker's hat
a hat that would not be out of place
in a production of *Waiting for Godot*.
No half smile of appreciation, not a word of thanks,
just more cruddy lyrics—
You are an eerie irritant
an irritation of extraordinary beauty...
In ten years I wouldn't be surprised
the raspy-voiced busker will be renowned
and playing fine halls and concert venues
but then I predicted the end of the world
on seven separate occasions
and was wrong six times.

The Night We Kissed Each Other Better
By
Matthew Hall

There is no overtime available in this particular job, which is just as well. Eight hours straight is long enough. Nine hours if you count the walk home. I could cut the journey by two thirds on the night bus, but I like the walk. I'm on better terms with the world when I'm walking. Once you get out of the city centre it's just you, your feet, and the concrete. And you get something of yourself back. Something stolen by the day's thievery. Besides, you have to be good and drunk before the night bus becomes a viable option.

I finish work at eleven. By the time I get into the heart of the city its jubilations are well under way. I side-step vomit, broken glass, spilt kebab meat and slimy onions. I weave in and out of clusters and crowds of revelers, keep my eyes to the ground and my collar up against my ears. I ignore the stretched limo hired by yet another crass hen party. They've downed all the champagne. Full of red bull and vodka they take turns to wave a huge inflatable penis out of the window.

Clucking.
Cackling.
Leering.
It's all so fucking boring.

It's all fancy-dress bar crawlers with a basic lack of imagination. Ill-fitting superhero outfits. A drunken Spider-Man forgets to remove his mask before doubling over to puke. Wonder Woman's skirt is tucked into her thong at the back. She's been pissing or fucking down an ally. Her ass would be cold if not for the Bacardi Breezers and Meow Meow. Catwoman has a warm fuzzy sense of satisfaction from observing the deep stretch marks embedded in Wonder Woman's big ass. Ironman and Batman are bickering over cab fare. In the coming week they'll look back and laugh as though life is theirs for the taking.

Sneering.

Scoffing.

Pretending.

It's all so fucking depressing.

A busker plays "Wonderwall" at the waterfront and the crowd sings along tunelessly demanding he play it again and again and again. None of them sling a quid into his hat. How does he do it? How does he carry that fucking smile?

Smiling.

Singing.

Playing.

It's all so fucking contrived.

I wait to cross the street in front of the aquarium where all the cabs clog up the road. They pick up fares there and turn around and honk their horns and rush about, incessantly yapping into their hands free phones. To my left a girl of around twenty-five sits on the paving slabs. Her legs are spread. She is rummaging through her purse. Her friend's puffy, blood-shot eyes, smeared make-up and streaked mascara, give away the tears she has cried earlier in the night. Behind me, up against the red brick wall of the aquarium, the third member of this trio is half-crouched, half-leaning. She has lost a shoe. Her Hello Kitty panties are twisted to the side. Her waxed pussy is exposed. I stare at it for a while. It looks so sad. Hurt somehow. And I feel an incredible weight of shame around my shoulders. Every pornographic image I have ever stared into flashes before my eyes. I see my ugliness reflected in all those tits and assholes and cunts.

Groomed.

Gaping.

Aggressive.

It's all so fucking terminal.

I want to get down on my knees and engage with her cunt. Find out where all the hurt and anger has stemmed from. I want to get past all the smut ingrained in me and really connect. I want to understand. I want to form a relationship with it. I want to stop objectifying it. I want to make eye contact. I want to show something of myself to it. We could share some kind of emotional breakthrough and that could erase all the impure memories from my mind. I should ask her to forgive me. I could offer to forgive her. If only I knew what it is we need forgiveness for.

"What happened to you?" I'd say on bended knee.

"Fuck off," the cunt would reply. She want's nothing to do with me. She closes her lips concealing and protecting her inner workings.

"Why so guarded?" I'd ask, desperate to share a moment with her.

"Leave me alone," she'd demand.

"I want to connect with you," I'd insist.

"Fuck off."

"So hostile," I'd say, slightly hurt by her general disinterest in connecting with me. Then I'd remember the first time I saw a cunt in a magazine. I'd relive the contrasting feelings of nausea and excitement. My heart would start pounding fast and hard. I'd be overcome by nervousness. Short, shallow breaths. Shaking. Sweating. Oh the guilt.

"I'll show you hostile," she'd snarl, licking her lips with a whip-lash tongue. She'd spit vaginal mucus into my face. She'd bare her sharp, yellow teeth and growl. I'd wipe my face with the cuff of my coat. I'd be persistent. I'd press on.

"I don't want to hurt you. I just want to understand." I'd remember my first time. I'd feel nostalgic for my virginity. I'd blush slightly as I pictured myself at age fifteen, aiming for penetration and failing. Why are pain and pleasure so intrinsically entwined? It was all so unnatural and confusing.

"Understand this you fucking moron. I bleed and weep for this bitch I'm attached to and how does she repay me? She pulls out my hair. She doesn't protect me. She makes prey of me. She's drawn to predatory types. Look at me. Look at her."

Drunk.

Docile.

Wasted.

It's all so fucking sad.

"I've played host to seventy-seven pulsating penises of varying shapes and size," the cunt would continue. "I've been through two abortions, one stillbirth and seven miscarriages. I'm a walking talking venereal disease. So what the fuck do you want from me?"

"I want to be your friend," I'd suggest.

She'd quiver slightly at the word "friend." I'd realise how little she knows of friendship. I'd realise how little I know of friendship.

Abandoned.

Alone.

Waiting.

It's all so fucking devastating.

I'd lean in close. I'd see her as she once was. Her hymen still intact. I'd see the way life had unfolded for her. I'd see her hopes and dreams shattered and trampled. And the sadness of it all would be too much to take in. I'd try but I wouldn't be able to absorb it. I'd lean forward and try to kiss her better. My lips grazing hers like a mating dance. Like butterfly wings. And all at once she would open up to me. I'd lose myself and find her. She'd let go and kiss me back. The whole world would stop spinning. Stop failing. And we'd fall with abandon and she'd be beautiful and I'd be beautiful and we would be beautiful together.

Grazing.

Gripped.

Melting.

And it's all so fucking beautiful.

Then the Hello Kitty panties were adjusted and the cunt was gone. I couldn't tell if she had caught me staring. I stepped out into the road hoping one of the cabbies would accelerate at just the right moment and kill me good and fucking dead.

The Third Way

By

Matthew Harrison

Roy Makepeace was hopeless with women. And he didn't fancy men. So when Androgynous Inc. came out with its "Third Way" line of androids, Roy was right up there for the first release.

Its revolutionary product notwithstanding, the company believed in the old-fashioned approach, and Roy actually had to queue at the entrance with other people. At least he assumed they were people. Most of them were men, edgy like himself, trying not to catch one another's eye or the attention of the circling media drones. There were also a few women, immersed in their mobiles. Above them animated posters proclaimed the virtues of the new line but no one looked up.

The doors opened, the queue shuffled along surprisingly quickly, and in no time Roy found himself in a meeting room with a personal counsellor. (It *was* an old-fashioned company.) To Roy's surprise, the counsellor was female – to be precise, a kindly, auburn-haired, motherly-looking woman – and this was awkward, for he did have certain *requirements*. But why be shy? He was rebelling against traditional notions of sexuality. Steeling himself, he said that he would like to try one of the new line.

"Yes, yes," the woman said briskly, "we're here to help you prepare for the experience. My name's Angie, by the way."

"Prepare?" Roy asked. "What do I have to prepare?"

"Wouldn't you want to prepare yourself for a new relationship?"

Roy was taken aback. "Er..."

"Exactly!" Angie beamed. "No one does. And that's the problem. Would you expect a doctor to practice without preparation?"

"No–o," said Roy, "but–"

"You see, your ideas are all tangled up," she went on. "Like here on your form you state, 'Must be tall,' but later you say, 'Petite preferred.' That's not consistent."

"I–I–"

Angie smiled at him, the auburn hair framing her face fetchingly. She was younger than he had first thought, around his own age and, confused though he was, Roy wondered if he should be writing off the entire female sex.

But Angie had become business-like again. "We'd better check your alignment. Here, just react naturally – be yourself." She motioned, and the wall behind her became a squirming mass of female flesh. "Hold it; one – two – three, you can relax. Now focus again," the wall showed two muscular grinning men, "that's it, relax."

Angie checked a screen in front of her. "Hmm. Not much reaction." She looked up with a professional smile. "It's seems that you *are* into "Thirdism," you're the right type for this product. Well, that's good!"

Roy struggled to get to grips with the situation. Couldn't he just choose and try at home?

"Is that how you would treat a new friend?" Angie

looked disappointed. "Try at home? Is that how to win someone's affection?"

It was harder to rebel against sexual norms than Roy had expected. This Angie was too intrusive. At last he said, "I am paying for this, you know."

"There you are – traditional male values!" Angie threw up her hands.

"But if it's any consolation," she went on, "our women customers are just as bad. Want to be treasured before they've put in any effort themselves."

"And you know what," Angie continued remorselessly, "they get away with it. Women get away with it. And men get away with it too!"

"What–What do you mean?" Roy stuttered.

"Men and women both hate the role their partners play in a relationship, but they have to accept it. And you know why?"

Roy did not trust himself to speak.

"Because if they choose another partner, it will be just the same!" Angie said triumphantly. "The classic monopoly. There's just one other sex!"

"And that," she concluded, "is where Androgynous comes in. We offer Thirdism – a Third Way. We are here not just to make money, not just to meet our customers' needs. We want to bring competition into a monopolised market." Her eyes shone. "We want to change the world!"

***

It was all overwhelming for Roy – not only the

preparation, but the actual choosing, which they went on to shortly afterwards. He found himself looking down into a glass-walled room that reminded him of a fish tank, around which strutted figures that were hard to make out in the brilliant light. Angie asked him which one he fancied, and numbed by the whole experience, Roy just pointed at random.

A moment later, he was standing in the lobby with the figure beside him, realising that he would now have to go out with her (with him?) alone. He stole a glance at the android. Nearly Roy's height, it was slender, with short-cropped hair – almost boyish (if one had to use conventional terms), but with a soft jawline and a curious plumpness about the hands. It was dressed in a sort of kaftan that avoided the question of sexual orientation.

Feeling slightly queasy, Roy wondered if he was making a ghastly mistake.

"Chin up!" Angie whispered to him, "Everyone feels a bit uncertain at first. Thirdism isn't easy. And don't forget, it'll be the same for *s*chmer."

"Schmer?"

"That's the pronoun for our Third Way product! Not he, she, or it, but schmer. It doesn't decline – 'I do it to schmer, schmer does it to me." Angie laughed. "Sorry, that was a bit out of court!"

Roy couldn't help smiling. Then he recalled his special requirements, but it seemed too crass to raise that now.

Angie led the way to the payment counter and Roy submitted to the confirmatory retinal scan. Then Angie shook hands with both of them. She squeezed Roy's arm and whispered, "You'll be fine." Giving the android a quick kiss, she waltzed back into the office.

Roy braced himself and turned to the android. Schmer's smooth oval face was impassive, its owner apparently absorbed in the still-lengthy queue beyond the glass doors. The face showed no connection to him at all.

For a moment, Roy thought of giving up. He could call Angie and her comforting presence all would come right. But this thought was overtaken by another. The android's indifference aroused a strange feeling. He found himself piqued. He *was* going to see it through.

"Come on," he said, "let's get home." Ignoring the curious glances from the queue, he took the android's plump hand and led the way along the street until there was space to call down the hovercar.

***

Later that evening, when Roy was alone again, he realised that Angie had a point. If he thought about his own motives for buying the android, they were indeed traditional – he wanted gratification without complication because, frankly, he wasn't competent to hold down a relationship with a real woman. He had tried female androids, the Tamagotchi ones, but even their limited responsiveness was too much. That was why he had reached out to Androgynous. The Third Way promised a fresh start.

And how did he feel now? How did he feel about…

schmer?

Roy gingerly examined his feelings. They were delicate, but there were elements of warmth.

The android had a name – Drew. Roy repeated it to himself, "Drew," and then louder, "Drew."

There was a stirring from the bedroom. "Yes?" came a husky voice.

The android was in there, supposedly asleep. "Sorry," Roy called. He went over and shut the bedroom door.

Talking earlier that evening, he had found Drew's personality surprisingly developed for someone formed only the previous week. It was, of course, all programming but as Roy questioned the android and heard answers in that husky voice, with details covering more than thirty years of notional life, Drew seemed more and more human. Roy found himself sharing painful experiences -- at school, that excruciating first date, the missed promotion – and receiving similar confidences in return, albeit steered delicately around the details of gender orientation.

In fact, so engrossed had Roy become in the android's life and their mutual sharing that his *requirements* had dropped from his mind. It was only when Drew yawned and mentioned bed that Roy rather embarrassedly came to. Drew must have the master bedroom. He bustled about making up the bed regretting the rather dilapidated state of his flat. He thought belatedly of pajamas, but realised he only had male ones, his own. That would be something to sort out the following day.

Yes, he thought, as he lay down in the spare room,

there was lots to be done – and lots to adjust to, as Angie had said. He found that he rather relished it. And when eventually his overloaded brain relinquished its grip on the day, it was Angie's kind face that accompanied him into sleep.

* * *

The next day, Roy and Drew went out to buy clothes.

There was, of course, no Third Way section in the local department store and Drew gravitated towards unisex teen fashion, although with much nose-wrinkling at the colours and the extravagant designs. The android would come out of the changing room in some jump suit or smock, asking, "How do I look?" and Roy, newcomer to Thirdism, responded as best he could.

Drew had just returned to the changing room when a matronly voice broke in, "That your little girl? They do grow up fast!"

Roy blinked; it was the shop assistant.

"But don't let her wear that," the woman continued as Drew reappeared in a loose flowery top, "the boys'll be all over her," and with a wink the assistant went back to folding clothes.

If the selection of clothing hinted at Drew's feminine side, other parts of the store called out the android's deeper nature. Roy was leading them towards Men's Clothing thinking vaguely that Drew might like something there, when Drew stopped.

They were passing Home Improvements. Roy

nodded, and they went in. Drew engaged the assistant in a detailed conversation about power drills. Finally they bought one "for household repairs," Drew explained, "you need it, together with a small knife."

"What's the knife for?" Roy asked. He was surprised again that Drew had such definite tastes and opinions.

"It's for you," the android said simply.

Touched, though it was hardly what he would have chosen for himself, Roy led the way out of the store holding a bunch of bags. Drew stepped lightly after him.

***

Roy was back at Androgynous for consultation after his first week with the Third Way.

"So how are you feeling," Angie greeted him. Roy saw that the auburn waves had been brushed a different way – and was that a hint of perfume?

But he was too full of himself and his new feelings to notice more. "The craziest things, you wouldn't believe," he began.

"Go on," Angie said, smiling.

"I took her, I mean, schmer, to a bar – and you know what happened there?"

"I can guess," Angie said, "but tell me."

"I was just thinking of us having a quiet chat, you know, when all of a sudden, a butch guy came over and asked to buy Drew a drink. He said," Roy repeated the words carefully, "'You don't want a honky like him,' – meaning, me – 'I know what you want.'"

"How did Drew react?" Angie said, a professional look coming into her eyes.

"She just said she was with me."

Angie nodded approvingly.

"And later," Roy went on, "Drew went up to the bar to get the next drink – I provided the money of course – and guess what happened there?"

Angie waited expectantly.

"The barmaid got chatty! And the woman sitting nearby pitched in too. It was like they were competing for Drew!"

"And how did you feel about that?" Angie said quickly. She had stopped smiling.

"I–" Roy stopped. How *did* he feel?

"Jealous?" Angie prompted, watching him closely.

Roy thought to himself. He *should* feel jealous. But heck – this wasn't about faking it. "No," he said frankly, "I didn't. More like... like, proud, I guess."

Angie didn't say anything but nodded to herself with seeming satisfaction.

Roy waited. Angie still didn't speak. "How am I doing?" he said at last.

Angie looked at him. "Roy," she said, "I think you're doing well. You seem to be dealing with things honestly, taking time to adjust, for both of you to adjust."

"Should I be going, er, faster?" Roy asked. "I mean, how long is it supposed to take before...?" The question seemed crude even as he uttered it, and he blushed.

"Just take as long as you need." Angie put a hand on his arm. "It is often like this with our clients – they come in with very high expectations, and they are perhaps not in the best emotional shape themselves. It all takes time."

"Sounds like therapy," Roy laughed.

"It does," Angie agreed. She rose and walked him to the entrance of Androgynous. In her high heels she was nearly his height. "Just call me if you need anything."

As Roy walked away, he thought it was no wonder Drew was so nice, coming from a good company like this. For almost the first time in his life, things were going right.

***

The good feeling lasted until Roy reached his apartment block. A humming noise was discernible as he entered the lobby, but he thought nothing of it until the lift opened on his floor, and then the noise hit him. They were demolishing his flat!

He rushed up to his front door, fumbled with the keypad, and got it open. At first he could not make anything out. A cloud of dust masked the room, and dimly he saw sheets draped over the furniture, a dark hole in the wall, a figure holding a drill.

"Drew!" he cried. "What are you doing!?"

The dust-covered figure lurched towards him, and Roy saw with horror that it was naked! He had time to make out a clutch of dark hair where the slender legs joined the body – and then Drew was upon him, the power drill whining dangerously. Roy jerked back in fear. Luckily the flex proved short, whipping the drill out of Drew's hand, whereupon it fretted itself into the floor and stopped. Drew collapsed and burst into tears.

Roy stood panting, conscious of the taste of the dust, glad to be alive. However, as Drew remained prone and sobbing, concern took over. Moving the drill out of harm's way, he knelt down and patted the dusty naked back along which the ridge of the spine showed prominently, murmuring, "There, there."

The sobbing eased. Roy fetched a blanket and covered the bare shoulders. Then he helped the android into the bathroom and ran the tap.

"I can manage now, Roy," Drew said, taking deep shuddering breaths.

Roy looked carefully at the android. "You nearly got me there," he said finally.

"I know. I'm sorry."

"But why, Drew? I wasn't going to hurt you."

The oval face puckered, and Roy thought there would be tears again. But the voice was firm. "It's the hormones, the cycles take a while to get into balance. They should have told you."

"Will it happen again?"

"I don't think so. My systems have tracked everything. It will settle down." Drew looked at Roy and smiled. "You know what set me off?"

Roy shook his head.

"Your knife. I felt threatened."

Roy was flabbergasted. "But the knife was from you!"

Drew looked down. "You don't understand."

"I certainly don't!" Roy retorted. But as the android

began sobbing again, he patted the towel-covered shoulders. "Get clean...get warm," he muttered, and went out into the living room to give the android privacy, closing the door behind him.

When he heard the sound of running water, Roy summoned his portable and connected. At the sound of Angie's voice, he began in a rush, "You are not going to believe this."

**

The following day Roy arrived at Androgynous with Drew.

"Now, I understand how you feel, Roy," Angie began in an official tone, as they were seated in her office. "After what you've been through, you certainly have the right. But I would ask you to reconsider."

"Reconsider what?" Roy said.

"I mean, not return your purchase," Angie said. "We would advise you to give it time, for your own good."

Roy blinked. "I'm not returning Drew." He turned to his companion. "Am I?"

Drew's face remained expressionless, but a plump hand stole into Roy's.

Roy squeezed the hand, and let it go. "What I'm really here for is clarification of how we're...how we're supposed to relate."

Angie seemed uncomfortable; she shifted in her seat. "I'm not really qualified for joint counselling."

Roy leant forward. "You know us both. You know

Drew, at least."

Angie relaxed. She nodded. "They're not with us very long, but we do take an interest. Like with one's own children. Not that I have any children," she laughed, "but if I had, I imagine I would feel the same way. We're glad when they find a good home."

"And I'm sure that you're a good man, Roy. That's why I recommended..." Here, something seemed to affect Angie's throat, and she stopped.

Roy waited as Angie pulled out a handkerchief and coughed. Then as she waved him to continue he asked what he and Drew were supposed to mean to each other. "Are we supposed to be lovers?" he asked, wincing as he said the word. "Or friends? Or what?"

Angie looked up, and to his further surprise her eyes were moist. "Roy," she said, "There is no, 'supposed'. Third-ism is something new for mankind, a new world. Just take it as you find it." She turned to Drew. "You too, dear."

Drew turned to Roy. "I think I'll step outside, I need a little air – still not quite balanced."

At Roy's anxious glance, Drew said, "I'm fine, fine, just a short break." And with that the android left the room.

Roy half-rose to follow, but Angie motioned him to sit down. "They're quite tough, you know, I shouldn't worry."

Roy sat back, still looking at the door.

There was a moment's silence.

"Well," Angie said, "is there anything more you want to ask me? Or shall I just wish the two of you happiness?"

"But that's just it!" Roy burst out. "I don't feel

anything like that for Drew."

Angie said nothing. Then, very gently, "How do you feel?"

"I feel – I feel like what you said-- for a child. I feel like a *father*."

Slowly, but with gathering confidence, he went on. "Oh, sure, Drew's crammed full of exo-memories, but they're all unformed, unsynthesised. Like with the drill – a teenage tantrum. Drew needs...you know, a parent."

He stopped, aware that Angie was looking at him intently.

"That's so sweet, Roy," she said. Then she coloured. "Sorry, I really shouldn't say that. Completely unprofessional."

"You know, Roy," she began again in a lower voice, "I'm really a bit of a failure at what I do. One does get *involved*."

Confused, Roy persevered with his line of thought. "So, I mean, do you have any advice?"

"I think you've advised yourself," Angie said. "You don't need anything more from me." Her lip trembled. "Do you?"

Roy looked at Angie and saw her, it seemed, for the first time. The wry sense came to him that, failure that he was in so much of his life, his rebellion against sexuality was also failing. Yet this was not about proving a point.

"I think I do need something," he said firmly. "Angie..."

The Man Above
By
Paul Rhodes

Lifting the ceiling panel and sliding it aside a couple inches, the light from the room below forces my eyes shut and I cover my face with a dusty forearm. Blinking into the stinging blur the scene beneath me comes into focus. The restaurant is half-full, busy for a Tuesday night.

Suzy is babbling as the waiter leads her to the booth I reserved for us at the back of the restaurant. Her words are inaudible from where I'm hidden but her eyes are wide and she's tugging at the hem of her dress.

Suzy orders a glass of wine and waits for the waiter to return, fidgeting wildly. Her fingers dart around her face - fondling her ear lobes, scratching her neck, dabbing at the end of her nose.

The waiter sets down the glass of wine and hands Suzy a menu.

"This is the Sauvignon Blanc, right?" asks Suzy. And then, before the waiter gets a chance to answer, "You've chilled it to the correct temperature haven't you? Does it pair better with chicken or fish? I mean, it's dry so I should drink it with fish, shouldn't I?"

"Um, sure, whatever you like," says the waiter, looking at Suzy strangely. "Should I wait for your date to arrive before I..."

"He's not my date," Suzy cuts in, "He's just...well, I

suppose he is, isn't he? I mean, I met him online but we've never really met...in person, so I guess this is a date isn't it? A blind date...although, is it really a blind date if you arrange it yourself?"

The waiter, unnerved by Suzy's rapid fire questioning, is backing away now sliding his notebook and pen into the breast pocket of his shirt. "I'll be back in a bit," he mumbles.

"Yes, sorry...thank you," says Suzy, her face reddening.

I watch her for a few minutes. She fiddles with her watch and checks her make-up with a small blue compact. Her hair is free from the tight bun that she usually wears and blonde curls fall toward her shoulders.

She takes a long pull on her glass of wine and runs her hands across her thighs, over and over, pushing out the wrinkles in her pale grey-blue dress. The same dress that I watched her buy from Lipsy yesterday evening.

My heart is in my mouth as I slide on to my belly, put my face to the crack in the ceiling and whisper, "Suzy, its Monty, your date - don't look up."

Immediately, Suzy looks up.

"Monty?" she gasps.

"No, no, no, don't look up!" I hiss, "Quick, pretend you're reading the menu."

Suzy grabs for a menu, scattering cutlery and sending the pepper-shaker sliding across the table.

Shrinking back into the shadows, I scan the restaurant until I'm sure nobody has noticed.

"Can I talk to you now?" asks Suzy, through gritted

teeth, wild-eyed, the menu pressed against her face.

"Wait – here put this on," I say, dropping a hands-free headset through the gap in the ceiling onto her lap.

Suzy fits the earbuds in and glances up at me, then quickly back down.

"Monty? What's going on? Am I going to get a phone call? Who from? Why on earth are you in hiding in the ceiling?"

"Just talk normally," I tell her, "There's no need to whisper. People will presume you're making a phone call – nothing out of the ordinary is happening."

"Nothing out of the ordinary is happening?" she yelps, "You're hiding in the bloody ceiling of Bella Italia! This is supposed to be a date!"

"I haven't been entirely honest with you, Suzy," I whisper. "I'm a 'Clandestine-ist.' I wanted to tell you, but I thought you'd find it too weird and wouldn't go out with me."

"A what? Why are you up there? Are you on the run? A fugitive? Have you killed someone? You're not a terrorist are you? Are you? Are you a terrorist, Monty?"

She forces her hands over her mouth and squeezes her eyes shut, muffled questions barely audible, "Mmmmmmmmmmmmmpppppphhhhhhhhhh?"

"No, nothing like that. Please, calm down and let me explain."

Suzy's taking huge breaths now, the air rasping as it forces its way out through her fingers.

"Please explain, Monty," she pants, "because right now I feel like getting up and leaving."

She takes another gulp of wine, and as she sets the glass down I can see her hands are shaking.

I let her sit there for a moment, watching as she takes long deep breaths; in through the nose, out through the mouth. Then as the panic starts to subside I begin.

"I guess it was the children thing that started it," I tell her, "all the sex..."

"Oh my God, you're a paedophile!" shrieks Suzy.

Now people are paying attention. Conversations are paused, cutlery is put down and heads are turned toward Suzy and the waiter who arrived at the table just as Suzy let rip.

Realising that the entire restaurant is looking at him, the waiter, drops of sweat beading on his forehead, turns to face the crowd of horrified diners.

"I'm not!" he shouts, his face contorted with horror. "She's not talking to me, she's on the phone, see? She's got earphones...I've done nothing with kids!"

And then he's gone, probably out into the kitchen where he's telling the other waiting staff to avoid serving the lunatic in the booth at the back of the room.

"Me neither!" I plead, as quietly as I can, hoping that Suzy can hear me. "Just listen to what I have to say, please, it's nothing bad, I swear!"

Suzy glares up at me, squinting into the ceiling. "You have two minutes," she says, "then I'm gone."

Suzy knows that I was married, I told her during one of our on-line chats. Technically speaking, I still am.

"Michelle, my wife, wanted a baby," I tell her. "We tried for months and got nowhere. We went to a doctor but he just told us, you're young, keep trying, it'll happen. After that, Michelle became obsessed. Before work, after work -- sex, sex, sex. She'd drive by my office at lunchtime so we could go do it in the car somewhere. I was exhausted-- mentally, physically – I didn't even enjoy it anymore."

"You had a lot of sex, I get it," Suzy snaps. "Don't worry, you'll not have that problem tonight."

"Seriously, I was a wreck," I continue. "She'd grind up Viagra and stir it into my tea so she could get a few more rounds out of me. Everywhere I went I'd have an erection. You should've seen the looks I got at our local swimming pool."

"Good evening, madam, would you like to order some food, maybe another glass of wine?" asks a different waiter, surprising us both.

"Oh yes, definitely another glass," says Suzy. "In fact, why don't you bring the bottle?"

"Can I get you anything else?" the waiter asks.

Suzy puts her hand over her mouth, pretending to cough, smuggling out the words "should I, *cough, cough,* order you, *cough,* something, *cough*?"

As fake coughs go, it's probably the worst I've seen.

The waiter, a tall pale lad with more hair gel than hair, looks concerned. *Maybe she is insane,* I can see him thinking.

"No, thank you, I think I'll eat later," says Suzy, when I don't answer. "My date...his train is delayed, we're just talking now," she says, tapping the earphone, "Just in case you were wondering who I was talking to.

And then, as the panic begins to rise and her face

fills with blood; "Were you wondering? Who I was talking to? Were you? Had you noticed? That I was talking, and there's nobody here with me? Had you noticed that?"

"Your earphone's not connected to your phone, madam," says the waiter quietly, with a sympathetic nod toward the unconnected lead and Suzy's phone, lying side by side on the table. "I'll go get the wine."

Grinning awkwardly, Suzy connects the lead to her phone.

Shifting around in the void, trying to get comfortable, I watch as the waiter brings the wine to the table and disappears into the restaurant.

"Can you just get to the bit where you tell me why you are hiding in the ceiling, please?" says Suzy. "I mean, I'm used to embarrassing myself, that's a regular occurrence, but I can't take much more tonight."

She sounds weary and sad. This is not the date she was hoping for.

"Michelle and I were shopping in Holland & Barrett, the health food store," I tell her, "here, at the Bluewater Mall. Michelle was buying Maca root or some shit. We go to pay and she asks the girl behind the counter if she could recommend anything for male potency. Seriously, this girl's like 17 years old. Michelle's telling her about our struggle to conceive and starts getting hysterical. Before long, we've got a crowd around us. People are patting my back, telling me it'll be OK, that I shouldn't be embarrassed. One guy tells me I need to eat eight bananas a day. Can you imagine that? Eight bananas! One kid even asked his Dad what a sperm count was! I wanted the world to swallow me up whole. People were yelling all sorts of shit – eat seaweed, trying warming your balls against the oven door first, lose weight, drink less alcohol…

"'I'm always telling him to cut down his drinking,' Michelle told the crowd, 'and he only drinks more!'

"That's when the crowd turned on me.

"'Shame on you,' someone shouted. 'Get another man,' said another. 'I'm single if you're interested,' said the manager of Holland and Barrett, who'd come to see what the ruckus was all about.

"That's when I ran out of the store, through the crowds of shoppers in the hallway, into the nearest bathroom where I locked myself in one of the toilet cubicles.

"I remember sitting on the toilet with my head in my hands. The voices from the crowd in Holland & Barrett rattling around my head like they were crammed in the cubicle with me.

"I imagined Michelle, marching around the Bluewater Mall searching for me, armed to the teeth with supplements, vitamins, more Viagra.

"I was desperate. I'm not religious but I looked up to God and asked for help. And then for some reason, I climbed onto the toilet, lifted one of the ceiling tiles and pulled myself inside.

"I replaced the tile behind me and lie up there in the darkness. I didn't move all day, except for when I climbed back down when the bathroom was empty and unlocked the cubicle door so nobody would figure out where I'd gone."

"How long ago was this?" Suzy asks.

"Just over a year ago," I tell her. "I've been living in the ceiling of the Bluewater Shopping Mall for just over a year...nearly 18 months actually."

Silence.

"Monty, I don't know what to say. You must have left the mall during that time...I mean; how have you been surviving?"

"The mall provides," I tell her. "I mostly sleep during the day and at night, when everyone has gone home, I climb down into whatever shop I choose and take what I need. The individual stores in the mall are locked at night but they are not alarmed."

"So you're a thief," says Suzy.

"It's not really stealing," I argue, "because I never take anything out of the mall. Think of it more as borrowing."

"But you're obviously taking food, Monty," Suzy says disapprovingly. "You're hardly borrowing that are you?"

"I earn what I eat," I tell her. "I watch out for shoplifters. When I find them cutting tags off designer clothes in the changing rooms, stuffing goods into their bags, I lean out of the ceiling, and politely advise them to stop. Scares the shit out of them, pretty funny really. I've saved the mall thousands."

"And no-one has ever reported you, Monty?"

"Nope, they've been caught stealing, what would

they say?"

"No, I don't believe it, you can't live like this. You must leave the mall, surely? I mean, you must, mustn't you? You couldn't possibly live like this? Could you? What about the CCTV? What about the guards? Monty? What about the guards...and the CCTV?"

Suzy's raving now, rattling off questions before she can remember if she's asked them already. The waiter approaches her for a moment, pauses, thinks better of it, and walks away.

"The CCTV isn't monitored at night," I say. "The mall is closed. What is there to look for? Security guards patrol occasionally, but only in the hallways, and the light from their torches gives me enough warning to hide."

"What about your wife?" Suzy asks. "She must have been worried sick. She probably reported you to the Police as a missing person?"

"I called her, a couple days after I disappeared," I tell her. "I told her I wasn't coming back and that she could do better – she didn't argue."

"And you're happy now?" Suzy asks, "Living in the ceiling?"

"Sure," I say, "I have no responsibility now, no obligations – I'm free."

"I'm not sure that you're free," says Suzy, "I mean, you're trapped, aren't you? In the mall? You have to hide don't you?" She takes a deep breath, "I mean, there can't be much space up there?"

"You'd be surprised," I say. "Inside the ceiling on each floor is void – dead space. I can crawl around the entire mall. It was designed that way so that maintenance guys can access the electricity or plumbing whenever there's a problem. I have a store guide so I know exactly which shop I'm above at any given time. Right now I'm living above Waterstones bookshop. It's awesome, like having my own private library."

"What else do you do here?" she asks.

"Most days I use the exercise equipment in House of Fraser – it's pretty well-stocked with treadmills and weights – it's as good as any gym I've been to," I answer. "I borrow DVDs from HMV and watch them on a 55" Sony TV in PC World. I've stashed a bean bag in the ceiling above the shop so I can bring it down for maximum comfort. As for food, I can recommend Marks & Spencer's luxury range; the beetroot and balsamic marinated salmon is to die for."

I notice the waiter approaching and slide back into the darkness.

"Madam, we're closing in about 30 minutes, can I get you anything else?" he asks.

"Just the bill, please," says Suzy, gazing past him. Her lips trembling with unspoken questions as her mind struggles to process all that I've told her.

"Very good," says the waiter with a relieved grin, "I'll be back in a moment."

"How do people usually react when you tell them this, Monty?" Suzy asks. "Because right now, I don't know what to think."

"You're the first person I've told," I say. "In fact, you're the first person I've spoken to in over a year."

Suzy's cheeks redden and she bites her lip,

desperately trying to suppress whatever string of questions is coming, and then; "Why me? Why me? Why me? Why me? Why me?"

"I saw you here a month ago," I tell her. "You were buying running shoes in JD Sports."

"Oh God," says Suzy. "You saw that?"

"I did," I say. "You started off asking if they were good for high arched feet, then you asked about marathon running, then cross-country running, then walking, and before long you were asking how old the kids were that stitched them together, how much they earned and where in Bangladesh the factory was."

"Shit," says Suzy, starting to fidget again.

"Another time I saw you ordering a sandwich in Subway – you were asking the questions before the sandwich kid could get a word in – What kind of bread do you want? Do you want it toasted? What kind of cheese? I saw how embarrassed you were when security threw you out – did you know they have a photo of you on the wall in their office?"

She sits there silent for a moment, scratching at her face and neck.

"It's a form of Tourette's," she says softly. "It comes on when I'm anxious."

"Don't be embarrassed," I tell her. "It's why I tracked you down. Being a Clandestine-ist can be lonely at times, but it's a lifestyle that I love and I'm ready to share it. I saw you and thought, who better to talk to than a girl that asks a lot of questions? We'll never run out of conversation! They've got all your details in the security office, so it didn't take me long to find you. I hope you don't mind."

"I should, but I don't," she says. "I'm actually quite flattered. The questions tend to put guys off, especially on movie dates."

"You should see the mall when everyone's gone, Suzy. It's like you're the only person left in the world," I say. "Clandestine-ism could be so much more than a lifestyle; it could be a movement - the next step in our evolution."

"How so?" she asks.

"Aren't you sick of it?" I ask her. "People staring at you when you ask all those questions, people sniggering? Struggling each day to fit into a society that rejects you?"

"I am," she says. "Sick to death of it. Trying to meet people's expectations can be so draining."

"People give so much of their lives away, Suzy," I say. "Uploading their thoughts for people they barely know to comment on. Putting it all on show for strangers - what they eat, where they go, who they fuck. Clandestine-ism is the antithesis to all that; give the bastards nothing, I say."

She looks up at me and I hold her gaze for a while, her hazel eyes searching deep within me, figuring me out.

"Can I stay tonight, Monty, just to..." she takes a deep breath and swallows hard, gulping down a question, "to see what it's like?" she splutters.

"I'd like that," I say. "Go to the ladies' bathroom and lock yourself in one of the cubicles, I'll come for you. I figured out how to run a movie in the theatre, we could go watch one – when the mall is closed of course."

"And if the questions start?"

"There'll be no-one there to shush you."

She smiles, a beautiful smile that makes me think that everything will be just fine. I hope so.

I allow my mind to wander for a moment and imagine a hidden society, living in shopping malls throughout the United Kingdom. A clandestine society that lives at the expense of a nation of consumers drunk with the obsession of having more than they need.

Suzy opens her purse as the waiter approaches with the bill.

"I'm sorry," I whisper. "I'd offer to pay for your wine, but we Clandestine-ists believe in a cashless society."

Never too Many Friends: Dumbshitism

By

Diane Arrelle

George eyed the long legged beauty sunning on the deck of the yacht. Eyed from a distance, of course, since he was in a small rented motorboat bobbing far enough away that they couldn't see he was spying on them. He made sure he looked like an early morning angler, a disguise he chose with great care, because no matter what he was going to come out of this with a new career. A career that awarded great perks like money, awe, and women by the score.

Tired of his life as a third rate gofer at the office, he decided he was going to become a private dick. He'd watched all the movies and TV shows. He'd spend his time reading the old pulp style novels. He fit the bill, almost. Like the heroes in the novels, he was disrespected, misunderstood, a loner, and yet a keen observer of others.

He'd overheard his coworkers referring to him as "a dullard, a loser, and a lost cause." Then there was the exceptionally loud, cruel, drunken conversation between two fellows at an office party who added to the insults, "a total waste of humanity and a bumbling blight on mankind."

It had hurt, but he was consoled because he knew different. Misunderstood summed him up nicely. And he was going to prove how good a dick he'd make by demonstrating that the woman on the boat was cheating on her husband.

43

So he sat, the rod propped between his knees and the long distance camera lens wrapped in his hands to keep down the sun glare glinting off it. He was so busy playing his version of Mike Hammer meets Magnum PI, he forgot to watch anyone else on the yacht. And he forgot to use the camera because he was so enthralled with the view. So enthralled, he forgot to notice anything else including the man with the rifle aimed at the motorboat. Ah, he always missed the little details.

George sat on the desert island where he'd been shipwrecked. He was chewing on a mango, a taste he had learned to loathe over the last two months, and contemplated his fate. That bastard had shot a hole in his boat, five holes in fact and as the small vessel slowly sank, George managed to get to this island.

Guess spying on Harvey's wife hadn't been such a good idea. He'd tried to convince the company vice president that his beautiful young spouse was bound to cheat on him. That kind of girl always did and Harvey was a hirsute gargoyle of a man with no redeeming qualities that George could see, except for money. The books he read never lied, beautiful broads who married short, squat, ugly men always did it for the money. Just a fact. He'd told Harvey as much and Harvey had laughed in his face.

"Details, Georgie. Give me the details."

George had been at a loss for words. He found that, although he was a keen observer, he missed the specifics. Probably his only real shortcoming. He planned to work on becoming more aware of the fine print in life, to dwell more on the details and improve his skill set. "Well Harvey, it's just the way it is. Everyone knows it."

Just as George was going to get those details on that gold-digger, Harvey shot out his outboard motor, planted three holes into the bottom of the wooden boat and then sailed close enough to George to yell, "Don't know why you are spying on me, but George you're fired."

George watched the water bubbling into the bottom of the small unseaworthy vessel and yelled back, "I just wanted to prove to you that I was right and that your wife was cheating. I was quitting anyway to become a private eye. I was doing this as a favor to you, a freebie."

"Well, you stink at it, but thanks anyway," Harvey laughed. "Next time when you are being inconspicuous on a stake-out, don't jerk off. Your boat was bouncing all over the place. Dead giveaway."

The small boat sank as the yacht sailed off, leaving behind one lone life preserver and a floating brochure to "Get Lei'd," an adult only Hawaiian resort.

George doggie paddled to the bobbing ring and rode it to the shore of this remote island. A short walk proved that the isle was small and the only things that grew on it were mangos and coconut palms. Luckily it rained a lot so he didn't die of thirst but the boredom was growing so intense he was beginning to wish he would.

Wondering for the millionth time, *what now?*, he spotted something glinting out beyond the waves.

He squinted and eventually the glint turned into a shine and the shine turned into a floating bottle. The bottle, pushed forward by the ceaseless waves, washed up onto the sand at his feet. He stared at it and wondered, *what now?*. Finally he kicked it away and to his utter surprise it rolled back to him. "Hmm, that's odd," he mumbled and kicked it again. It rolled back. He picked it up and tried to look inside but the bottle appeared to be filled with swirling smoke.

"Hmm, that's odd," he mumbled again not used to talking anymore. He twisted the lid and the bottle grew hot in his hands. So hot, he dropped it and as it hit the ground the lid popped off and the smoke in a rainbow rush gushed out of the bottle and a huge man stood in front of him.

"I am the genie of the bottle and you have one wish."

"Uh," George said. "Why you dressed in a tropical shirt and flip flops?"

"Cuz I got thrown off a cruise ship a few years back. My bad luck I ended up here with you."

"Bad luck? Good luck for me. A wish, huh? Say aren't I supposed to get three wishes?"

The genie sighed. "Look bub, I don't want to grant you any but rules say I gotta. Consider it the effect of inflation. Now you gonna make a wish or what?"

George opened his mouth to make his wish when the genie interrupted him. "Don't waste my time wishing for more wishes. You get one wish, you make it stupid and try to trick me I get mad. You don't want me mad. Now, make that wish. I want to get back inside, I was watching season three of Game of Thrones on Netflix."

George snapped his mouth shut. The genie had ruined his plan to get more wishes and in doing so issued a challenge. *I'm going to put this buffoon in his place*, he thought, and *somehow get even with Harvey for putting me in this damned predicament.*

He laughed and said, "OK, why not?"

"One catch, after you make that wish, it takes about a minute to work, so I need you to make sure I get a good long break this time. Bury my bottle in the sand of this deserted isle so it doesn't show. I want a really long vacation this time."

George smiled. Now he had his revenge for the lazy bastard. All he had to do was make sure he asked for everything he wanted in one sentence and to make sure he got all the details correct.

"I wish to leave this damned island, live in a real tropical paradise, sleep on clean sheets, never be lonely again, go to bed with countless women and make sure I'll be a real pain in the ass to Harvey."

"Granted, now bury the bottle."

The genie swirled back into his glass home and George capped it. Wading out knee deep into the water he buried it halfway into the wet sand so the top half sat under the water hidden from sight, just like the genie asked, but sure to be dislodged by the tide in a short time and set afloat again."

George didn't even have time to laugh at his clever betrayal of the genie because suddenly he was a tiny insect in a packed suitcase swarming with bedbugs.

"Hey, George," a hundred voices piped up. "Welcome aboard! You're just in time because we're leaving this New York hotel today and flying to a nice resort in Hawaii to live forever and ever!"

"Ah shit," George sighed in disgust realizing he'd gotten everything he asked for. "Damned details got me again. Guess I wasn't specific enough again after all."

Dark Signals

By

Essel Pratt

My lungs burn as I inhale the cigarette forcing the toxic carcinogens to sieve through my lungs and into my bloodstream before exhaling the remnants of the poison. The unfiltered cylinder, or cancer stick as my ex-wife used to say, bites at my begrimed fingertips as I draw away the last possible morsel of its existence. Nothing beats a good cigarette to help me relax after a long day, maybe it is night, of searching the dark signals for messages from beyond.

I'm not exactly sure where beyond is, who resides there, or why they relay cryptic messages to anyone that may chance upon their consistent banter. I only know that they are persistent in their attempts to transmit messages to whoever the intended receiver may be. So many have become predictable, yet I tune in to listen each and every time. It has become an obsession, I suppose. Yet, when I hear a new one, my heart pumps with adrenaline as I listen intently at the opening act, waiting patiently for the cryptic message that follows, and the grand finale sign off at the end.

I lean back in my once plush office chair staring at the cobwebs upon the ceiling waiting for the next numbers station to appear between the squelches of space and the plethora of foreign stations that emanate from my shortwave radio's speakers.

Pulling another cancer stick from the pack within my breast pocket, I inhale the fresh taste of tobacco leaves prior to lighting up. At times I have considered chewing on the tobacco, it would probably be better for my lungs, but the burn is half the rush of the shallow intoxication they coerce in my head.

The shortwave radio serenades me with a prayer station originating from Pakistan, a far distance from my Indiana home. There is something soothing about the voices, almost haunting to an extent. I'm not a religious man by any means, but the melodic reverence somehow relaxes me in a peculiar way. However, I don't allow the station to stay on for long, worried that a subliminal threat will draw me in to devote my existence to the false god that they pray to. I'm not saying they are wrong in doing what they do; it's just not for me.

I hit the scan button on my shortwave and pour a cup of coffee, only half way into the oversized mug, satisfying the rest with a cheap whisky. It takes away the shakes and the tremors. I sit back and sip on the cocktail, swishing it around upon my tongue, cleansing my teeth with the germ killing alcohol. I used to despise drinking and smoking, but this is life at the moment.

The scan of radio waves lands on an Egyptian frequency, one I have heard time and time again. The man within the broadcast always seems anxious and abrupt, spilling warnings of doom and gloom without the luxury of taking a much needed breath of fresh air. I often wonder if he knows what it is like to be half way between death and life, to be stricken with cancerous burden. Yet, I realize I don't care what he thinks or feels. He is just a faceless voice amidst the airwaves destined to live his life without knowledge of my existence.

I light my cigarette and press the scan button again, illuminated by the soft glow of the radio's monitor. The days and nights have become one within the darkness as I hide from society, determined they forget I exist until my cold body is found within the crypt that I have locked myself within.

I take a long hard drag, feeling the smoke enter my lungs and tingle me to a cough. Depression was once a phase of the diagnosis. Now I can only say a hearty *fuck you* to the damnation that has been cast upon my soul.

I close my eyes and take a swig of my medicated coffee, trying not to think of the demons that tempted my wife to leave with our kids. The same demons that riddled my body with cancer and the same devils that introduced me to the number stations. But they are always there lurking, taunting, and reminding me that I am a piece of shit that deserves everything that came my way. Fuck them.

Morse code, followed by atmospheric noise, and then a Russian radio station aired by the government. Each cycle through the airwaves, finally stopping on an American baseball game. Listening on shortwave radio frequencies always makes a sports game feel like I am sitting in front of the radio as a kid in the 50's. The nostalgia is peaceful, a reminder of simpler times, but also a reminder of the hellish life I live now. I press scan again.

Foreign banter fills the air-- from South America to

China, the same government bullshit fills the waves. If there is one thing I've learned over the past few years of hiding out within the darkness, it's that no matter where you live, life is full of conspiracy and damnation. Maybe my impending death isn't a curse, but a blessing instead.

The dial, the entire shortwave is digital but old habits and terms are hard to break, lands on a station that seems out of place. Out of habit, I begin recording the sound hoping to capture the cryptic message and save it with the others, comparing and contrasting the content, determined to translate and understand before I die.

A garbled voice speaks in tongues, sending shivers up my arms. It is unlike any other I have heard before. I feel a tinge of fright within my heart, an extra beat in between those that normally exist. I switch from USB to LSB, FM, and AM, but the signal comes through best over USB, so I return to it quickly, hoping that I don't miss anything important.

The demonic grumbling continues onward for three minutes and 32 seconds, filling my body with anxiety as each undecipherable syllable remains within my soul, biting at my nerves, and mocking my disease. Discovering a new numbers station always fills me with excitement. This one is scaring me, so far.

The airwaves go silent and I chug the last of my whisky tainted caffeine hoping to calm myself down a bit. My cigarette burns away in the ashtray, disappearing into a cloud of smoke, ironically similar to the fate I have accepted. I grab the cig and imbibe away at its life, taking from it what cancer is taking away from my existence.

I close my eyes and stare into the nothingness behind my lids, feeling the dull pain of alcohol and nicotine intoxication beat at my skull. It reminds me that I am still alive, barely, unlike the lethargic state my cancer meds and chemotherapy placed me into. I don't consider it giving up; instead I am taking control of my own fate.

As I sit in silence, the demonic voice arrives again, saying a few words in a language that may not be meant for human ears, leading into a distorted song that sounds eerily familiar to the Russian national anthem, yet different enough that I know that is not what it is.

I sit forward in my chair staring at the radio's digital screen anticipating what comes next, straining my eyes against the bluish luminescence. The song continues for two minutes and 19 seconds, intermingled with an oddity of screams that sound like lost souls screaming for release from the purgatory they are confined within. I feel my heart race as I grab the bottle of whisky and drink straight from the bottle attempting to wet my cotton filled throat. It is a numbers station I have not heard before, obviously new, because directly after the last note of the song, a clip from the newest popular television show quotes something about the family business and hunting. I double check to ensure I am recording the broadcast, anxious to play it back later.

Again, the airwaves go silent, not uncommon with a number station. My labored breath bellows out into the room. I take a long drag on my cigarette and feel dizzy. The toxic smoke enters my lungs and I cough, spitting blood onto the desk in front of me. I pull my sleeve over my hand

and wipe the splatter away, washing down the rest of the rusty crap with the last of my whisky. I should have brought another downstairs with me, like I need any more to drink.

The silent anticipation is driving me nuts. I begin to wonder if I may have misidentified the signal. Maybe it is just cross interference; maybe my imagination is giving in to insanity. Dammit, what if I've missed another numbers station broadcast. I slap my head, alternating between hands, half trying to beat away the fogginess that has invaded and half to occupy the silence that is booming across the concrete walls that surround me.

"Whiskey...Echo...Lima...Charlie...Oscar...Mike...Echo...Dos...Seis...Seis...Seis...Hotel...Echo...Lima...Lima..."

The letters and numbers repeat as the little girl on the other side of the dark airwaves shares the secret code, starting out sweet and innocent, almost cute; each subsequent repetition is more hollow and soulless. I listen for at full minute, finding myself repeating along with the little girl in unison with her tone. Another minute passes. My heartbeat begins to pump in time to the rhythm of her voice.

"Whiskey...Echo...Lima...Charlie...Oscar...Mike...Echo...Dos...Seis...Seis...Seis...Hotel...Echo...Lima...Lima..."

Anxiety surges through my nerves as I continue to stare at the monitor, my gaze affixed to the sound waves that visualize the damned voice. With each passing reprise, the decibel levels increase, garbling the sound under the uncontrolled squelching. I cannot look away as the voice crescendos.

"Whiskey...Echo...Lima...Charlie...Oscar...Mike...Echo

o...Dos...Seis...Seis...Seis...Hotel...Echo...Lima...Lima..."

My heart is hurting, like an unknown force has grasped the muscle and is squeezing it with every expansion. Pain radiates through my chest, veins in my forehead filling with blood as my heart refuses its entry. My arms and legs tingle with pricks of a needle and my eyes pulsate with pain as redness clouds my vision. Then, as the voice becomes unrecognizable, it repeats a final time in the innocent voice that it started with.

"Whiskey...Echo...Lima...Charlie...Oscar...Mike...Ech o...Dos...Seis...Seis...Seis...Hotel...Echo...Lima...Lima..."

As the voice diminishes to nothingness, all of my pain disappears. My breath is heavy and my sight is dim, but I find myself still staring at the screen, the sound waves flat lined. The timer on the recording shows that ten minutes have passed. I am still trying to catch my breath, my chest still tense and tight, my arms and legs weak.

I light another cigarette just as the Russian anthem begins to play, signaling the conclusion of the broadcast. Once again, the burn fills my lungs and I feel alive, as live as I can feel as life creeps toward its terminal velocity while cancer eats away from the inside out. I let the smoke leave my lips, inhaling it back through my nose, purifying it in my lungs once more. Damn, I really wish I had some more whisky, maybe some rum.

I hold my breath until the voice that began the broadcast begins to sound again. I blow out smoke rings into the air, watching them fade into nothingness. The voice frightens me, sends shivers down my arms, makes me anxious, and makes me want to turn off the shortwave radio. Instead I listen. I stare at the monitor, eyes affixed on the screen, watching the sound waves. They are different than before, their peaks and valleys don't seem to match the pitch of the voice, they are scattered and jumbled.

The voice continues though, speaking in tongues. I feel it is speaking to me directly and my heart begins to race once again. I can feel the cells within my body tingle, focused in the areas where the cancer has invaded. There is a lot of pain, but I feel numb to it all.

The image on the monitor becomes shaky and unstable, like a loose wire is being jiggled, but the room is still. The sporadic peaks and valleys begin to converge, maybe it is the redness in my eyes creating an illusion or a mirage, if there is even a difference. The sound begins to fade to nothingness, but comes back in full force, louder than I thought the speakers could even release. A demonic face appears where the sound waves should be, only for a split second and it vanishes.

I clutch my chest; the pain is worse than it has ever been. The frequency changes to an Islamic prayer, melodic and beautiful. The pain spreads to my shoulders and my arms. The channels scan again, stopping on a Hindu prayer, also beautiful in it foreign content. My body begins to seize, my tongue clamped between my teeth, blood rushing down my chin, pooling on my chest. The channels scan again, stopping on a southern preacher, spouting out damnation among his fire and brimstone lecture. I fall to the floor, my office chair flipping out from beneath me. My entire body burns in pain, helpless to call for help as I lay on the floor while my body tremors until the entire world goes black around me. Everything seems to stop all at once. I fade to nothingness, the excruciating burn remains as the last sound I hear escapes the speakers from the shortwave radio, clear, but echoing within my skull.

Matthew 7:13

"Enter through the narrow gate; for the gate is wide and the way is broad that leads to destruction, and there are many who enter through it."

Elixir Vitae
By
Edward Ahern

Frankie Witt crawled out of a stupor and into a hangover. The crust inside of his mouth crumpled like a wasp's nest as he squinted and staggered up. *Aghh. Head cracked open. Drink, gotta have a drink. No, too dried out. Water first, then booze.*

Frankie shambled into the bathroom, drank a glass of off-color water and weaved into the kitchen area of his one-wide trailer. The sink and counter top were overgrown with dirty dishes and food remnants. *Eat or drink?* His empty stomach chorused the agony in his head. *Both.*

Where's the blender? Frankie's eyes crawled over the mess. *Aha!* He grabbed the blender, and sloshed water into it, brightening the Margarita scabs inside it.

Put the vodka in last, don't waste what's left. He tossed in a vintage pizza slice, two dried-out hot dogs, and mildewed strawberries, topping up with a slug of the brownish water and a half pint of vodka.

The blender complained, sparking, but ground out a dung-colored mix. Frankie ignored the bubbles forming in the slush and swallowed a mouthful from the blender. *Ouph! Damn that's nasty. Alum and mold.*

His sinuses reflated like they'd been stented, and Frankie felt snot slithering down toward his throat. He was blowing his nose on a stained paper towel when his guts and muscles cramped and he dropped to the floor.

Frank Witt Dossier, NSA field excerpt: The well water is contaminated with animal fecal matter, microorganisms and lead from the piping. Unfortunately, none of the biological contents of the blender remain for analysis, the blender having baked in the desert sun when Mr. Witt tossed it from the trailer. Analysis of the residue revealed traces of arsenic, gold and mercury in addition to the expected levels of lead, iron, and calcium. Twenty-seven unclassified microorganisms were discovered on the food remains in the trailer kitchen, as well as two previously unknown species of fly.

Frankie came to three hours later. He cringed, then realized that nothing hurt. *Thirsty. Hungry.* He stood up without staggering, turned on the tap and drank directly from it. *Starving. But feel great. Great! Food. Nothing here I want to eat. No money to buy food. Take care of this tonic first.*

He began rinsing out the tequila bottle. The back of his right hand swung into a rusty steak knife, the blade penetrating almost through his palm. Frankie cursed at the pain, pulled his hand away, and stared as the wound stopped bleeding and closed back up. In three seconds there was nothing on his hand but a faint pink mark. *Sweet Jesus Murphy! Must be the DT's.*

Frankie pulled the steak knife out from the dish pile

and stared at it. The blade left smears of his blood on his fingertips. *I wonder.* He took the knife by its handle and jabbed it into and out of his left palm. Blood welled out for a second and then the skin healed over.

He poured the contents of the blender into the tequila bottle and recapped it. Then he put on pants, a T-shirt, and shoes, and walked through the trailer park and across the road to Bernice's Oasis, a bar masquerading as a diner.

Two all-day drinkers were perched at the far end of the bar. Bernice Sanders stood at the other end, shifting her attention between her cell phone and a shopping channel on the television. "I didn't think you'd make it this time, Frankie."

"Bernice, I'm starving. Please, a burger and fries?"

"And you don't have any money."

"Please, Bernice."

"You already owe me two hundred," she sighed. "Hell, all right. Better food than booze. Maybe I won't have to sell your liver to a freak show."

Frankie set the tequila bottle on the bar, the gelatinous contents quivering. "Okay, nothing for nothing. I'll give you a shot of this stuff. It's incredible what it'll do for you. Once you see how good you feel you'll wipe out the two hundred."

"Two-o-five counting the burger. Get that slimy looking filth off my bar, I'm not drinking it."

Frankie looked her over. During his two years in the bar Bernice had transmuted from solid to zaftig, hard to budge physically and conversationally. *This stuff is the* *water of life. I should be charging $2,000 a pop, not $200.*

"Okay, Bernice, you win. But I want to show you something before you cook up that burger."

Frankie took a folding knife out of his pocket and, without hesitating, sliced a line down his right forearm.

"You rotted-out alkie! You've lost it."

He said nothing, holding the arm over the bar so Bernice could watch the wound close.

"Well, jack up my sagging tits!"

Frankie pushed the bottle toward her. "Please, Bernice, you'll feel better than you have for a long time. Better sit down first, though."

"Not a chance, Frankie. You'll probably be running from both ends in a couple minutes."

Bernice delivered a burger, fries and beer to a table and sat quietly with him, working things out. "That's some brown slime you got here, Frankie."

"Yeah. I've been thinking too. There's maybe three quarters of a quart in the bottle. If I'm stingy, that's twenty shots. I should be able to get five, maybe ten grand a shot, easy. Problem is, I don't know people who've got that kind of spending money."

She patted his arm, avoiding the mark left by the knife. "You know I do from before, but consider Frankie, if that stuff works, your golden goose will dump twenty eggs and then you're out of income."

Frankie could sense relays clicking in his mind amazed that he could again think more than two steps ahead. "Yeah, and if I get the government to believe me, they'll confiscate the bottle, lock me up as a lab rat, and bleed me every so often." He exhaled slowly, calculating.

Bernice went behind the bar, poured a triple shot of cheap scotch, and brought it back. "Here, your hangover must be pushing your eyes out onto your cheeks."

"Thanks. It's weird, but this is the first morning in months that I haven't felt like a bad death." Frankie downed the drink in four swigs and frowned. "There's no pop, no jolt. It's like the stuff is neutralized as it's running down my gullet."

"You want another?"

"Don't think it'll do any good. Look, Bernice, I need someone like you to front for me, to be a cutout from the buyer. Here's the deal. You become like my agent, ten percent for helping set things up."

Her smile stretched almost to her jaw line. "Crap. Fifty percent or no deal."

"Sugar, don't rely on our two-backed beast act, this is business."

"Look, Frankie, I've got almost no money and you've got none. You're going to need cash to get rolling, which means selling a shot or two. But the people I know, first thing, they see this works, they'll want to muscle in, maybe take the bottle. You've got to be smart to play on their turf. Got to sell this stuff like a street drug. You only know booze."

"Okay, fifteen percent."

"Twenty five."

"Twenty, and you'll still have the option to get a shot."

"Done."

They didn't bother to shake the hands that'd previously explored each other.

"Run my tab up a little further?"

"What the hell."

"Bottle of Cuervo to take home. And an empty mini with a cap. Need to figure out how to stash the mixture."

"I gotta big safe."

"No offense, Bernice, but hiding this is my secret."

Bernice pulled the bottles from behind the bar and handed them to Frankie, then watched him walk away. *Two Cuervo bottles. Is he smart enough to work a switch? Not Frankie. Oops, not the old Frankie. This guy knows when to change his underwear.*

Frankie surprised himself by setting the real tequila bottle down unopened. *Don't think I can get smashed anymore, and that's all I know how to do. Think, you drunk, how are you going to handle this stuff?*

He went into the bathroom and knelt on the floor next to the toilet. Opening his knife, he pried up a floor tile. The tile had been glued to a same-sized section of the plywood flooring underneath it. Next to the opening the toilet drain pipe ran down through two feet of air and into the ground.

He pressed his cheek against the base of the toilet bowl and reached down through the hole, knife in hand. He scraped off an inch of dirt and animal droppings, then pulled his arm back out of the hole and dropped the knife. He stuck his arm back down and grabbed the screw cap of a five inch diameter PVC tube. Frankie wiggled the tube back and forth to enlarge its hole, then pulled the tube up through the floor hole.

Sweat dripped down his body, moisturizing a five day accumulation of drinker's body odor. He unscrewed the cap, dropped the Cuervo bottle into the tube, and screwed the cap back on. Frankie shoved the PVC tube back into its hole, and scraped debris back over the tube cap. He looked pensively at the result, then grabbed a paper cup, scooped water from the toilet, and sprinkled water over the disturbed dirt until he couldn't tell any difference from its moldy surroundings. *Time to celebrate.* He opened and nipped from the bottle. *I thought so, doesn't have any more kick.*

Frankie found some soap and showered and shaved. The rusty razor blade nicked him several times before he was done. He chuckled with every nick, watching the cuts snap shut.

His clothes were all soiled. He wrapped everything in a sheet and walked outside and over to the laundry room trailer, then paced back and forth naked until the machines were finished and he could put on something clean.

He wanted to walk back to the diner, but his system started shutting down. *Almost can't move. Okay, change of plan. Sleep.*

The banging on his door woke him up. "Frankie, get your skinny ass out of bed."

Frankie pulled on pants and opened the door to see Bernice, red faced and sweaty in the desert heat. "Jesus, Frankie, its eleven in the morning. I got news. Put a shirt on and come over to the diner."

The diner's air conditioning whacked Frankie as he

entered. Goose bumps started popping, but within two seconds they disappeared and he felt comfortable. *Man, I got a professional grade thermostat now.*

"Talk to me, Bernice."

"Okay, I made some calls last night while you were passed out. Nobody believed me, but one guy, Harry Clinton. He owes me a favor and says we can seem him at three. Then I fired up the laptop and put in some search words. Frankie, you wouldn't believe how many thousands of flaky web sites there are. So I went really specific on the search and answered some questions on a couple sites that looked sane."

"You didn't tell them where we are did you?"

"Come on, I'm the smart one, remember? I just lurked. Well, maybe a hint or two. We gotta go if we're going to make the meeting on time."

"Where'd you set it up?"

"A little restaurant I know."

Frank Witt Dossier, DEA excerpt: None of the adult males reputed to be part of Mr. Harry Clinton's crime organization admitted to knowing Miss Sanders and Mr. Witt, nor even to knowing Mr. Clinton. In sum, they admitted nothing at all.

It was little, with only nine tables. Three p.m. was too late for lunch and too early for dinner, so except for the waiter, the only people in the restaurant were the two men waiting for them.

Frankie focused in on them. *Middle aged, fat packed*

on muscle. Shirts hanging out over their pot bellies. Careless, they're not checking to see if anybody else is around.

Bernice and Frankie sat down wordlessly.

"You Bernice?"

"Yeah. Where's Harry?"

The talker of the pair tapped back half a glassful. "Harry sent us, says you gotta convince us before he'll talk to you. Where's this weird drink? And who's the drunk?"

"He's Frankie. And it's real. We got a drink makes you feel like you're screwing a seventeen year old cheerleader. And not only that. Show 'em Frankie."

"Hello." Frankie said. "Watch this." He reached in his pants pocket and pulled out the folding knife. Both men moved their right hands under their drooping shirts and belly flab.

Bernice let out a strained laugh. "No, no, relax. This is a demonstration."

Frankie slowly opened the knife and sliced a one inch cut in his forearm. He turned the forearm so both men had a good view. They watched as, in less than three seconds, the bleeding stopped and the wound closed. "We think it's permanent," Bernice said. "One drink and you're set. I knew Harry would doubt me, so I told him he could down the shot and pay me five large when he sees that it works."

Two burly necks twisted as they glanced at each other. The talker answered. "Harry says different. He says you give us the shot of this stuff for free. He likes it, he talks to you about how much you get when you give him the rest."

66

Bernice kept his eyes on the two men, but she could feel Frankie's presence. "That's not what he said. I'll call Harry again and explain things. Don't take it the wrong way, but no deal."

The talker leaned forward and backhanded Bernice across the face, splitting her lip. "Look bitch, we're doing it our way or you're going to take a beating you won't be able to heal from."

Frankie leaned forward, taking the mini bottle out of his pocket and showing it. "Look guys, let's just talk." As he was saying this he grabbed a plate from the table top and slammed it into the talker's mouth. The plate snapped in half and Frankie swung the jagged edge across the mute's throat.

"Holy frig!" Bernice yelled.

The two obese men fell out of their chairs and hit the floor. Frankie grabbed his own chair and bounced it off the two men's heads. "That didn't work out so well, Bernice." He unscrewed the mini and drank it. "Not for you, suckers."

The waiter had run back into the kitchen. The two fat men on the floor weren't moving. Bernice's eyes swung back and forth "Are they dead? Harry's gonna kill us both."

"Don't think they are, and that may be hard to do. We've got a few minutes before the cops come. Go through their pockets."

"Huh?"

"Chances are they brought the money just in case."

Bernice dropped to her knees, rolled the fat mute guy over and found his back-pocket wallet. "Must be three, four large here."

"Great. What about our other buddy?"

She crawled over to the other man, trying to ignore his splintered teeth, and reached down into his front pockets. "Got it. Exactly five grand. And they're both breathing."

"Check the back pockets too. He'll have money on his ass."

She found the wallet. "Yeah, another couple thousand. Here's all the money."

"Okay, gotta go." He took the money, then helped Bernice up, taking her arm as they walked to the car. "I'll drive."

Ten minutes into the drive Frankie glanced over at her. "Harry's people will be at your diner in a few hours. Repack your trousseau into the hope chest, we need to leave before they get there."

"They'll trash the place."

"You insured?"

"Yeah."

"Okay."

As Frankie began to crest the last hill before the diner and trailer park he spotted a large sedan parked in front of the closed diner, and three men in suits standing near the door. "You expecting anybody?"

"Nope."

"Suits in the desert. It's looking like Uncle Sam wants me. You must have gone "True Confession" on the web sites. I'll stay hid up here and watch you walk down like a beauty contestant."

"You abandoning me?"

"No way. But you can find out what they want. Go ahead and tell them the truth, except for the part about beating and robbing Clinton's men."

The three suits circled Bernice as she approached her diner.

"Bernice Sanders?"

"Yeah?"

"We need to ask you some questions about your web search last night."

"And who the hell are you?"

The three men flashed identity cards.

"They look different from each other."

"Joint task force, NSA, FBI, and DEA. Agents Withersi, Haunchez and Greune. How did you get here?"

"My chauffeur just quit."

The men exchanged glances, but knew they had no real chance of finding a driver in an unknown car. The shortest guy spoke. "Shall we talk inside?"

Twenty minutes after the questioning had begun, the diner's wall phone rang.

"Okay if I answer that? Might be important."

"Okay."

Bernice got up, walked behind the bar, and uncradled the phone. It was Frankie.

"Hi sweetie. Put one of them on, please."

She turned to them. "It's for you."

The FBI man in the middle got up, walked over, and took the phone from her. "Hello?"

"I'm the guy who drank the elixir. I've got more for

you, but you've got to do something for me."

"Keep talking."

"In about a half hour, a car full of large men will pull in and begin to threaten Bernice. If you hide in the kitchen with no lights on you'll be able to see and hear their threats, so you can arrest them for assault. They work for Harry Clinton. I'll give you what you need, but you make very sure that Harry knows to lay off. She gets hurt, you get nothing."

"And you're jerking me around. Come back here so we can talk."

"You looked sweet in that dark suit, but I don't think you're my type."

"Where's the substance? What's your name?"

"I'll call back in a couple hours. If Bernice tells me you took care of the posse, I'll tell her where you should look. Put Bernice back on, please."

"Frankie?"

"Sweetie listen. Tell these guys everything you know. Everything. Chances are they'll drug you and get the answers anyway. They're supposed to take care of Clinton's boys for you. I'll call back in a couple hours and make sure they did. Then I'll tell you where I put the Cuervo bottle. I called a TV station and tipped them that federal agents were arresting Clinton's goons. They'll maybe get there before I call. Busy, busy, gotta run. Later."

"Frankie? Frankie?" She dropped the phone back onto its hook.

"Okay, here's the whole story, no crap."

Forty five minutes later a silver gray Escalade pulled into the lot. Four men got out and walked into the diner.

Twenty minutes later the four same men were escorted out in handcuffs and put, two apiece, into back seats. The TV crew had just arrived, and, with no access to the diner and no real idea was going on, began filming the squirming men in handcuffs.

When the phone rang the DEA agent picked it up.

"Hello?"

"Is this Hello of Hello and Company? Aren't you supposed to announce yourself as Agent Sterling of the Incorruptible Agency?"

"Don't try and goad me, we've still got your girlfriend."

"Oh yeah, her. Put Bernice on, please."

"Where is it?"

"Ah, so something's checked out for you. In good time, once I've talked with her. It won't take long."

The agent waved Bernice over and held the phone away from her ear so he could listen in.

"Frankie?"

"Are Clinton's thugs taken care of?"

"Yeah."

"Is he breathing heavily on your cheek?"

"Yeah, but he's an Altoids addict."

"Good, a conference call. Okay Mr. Fed, the TV lice have been given Bernice's name, and warned that you'll try and kidnap her. I've retained a lawyer who'll be calling Miss Sanders shortly to make sure that her civil rights aren't being violated.

"Really, Frankie?"

"Yeah, Johnny Biden, the one the bail bondsmen

71

use. He seemed happy to get honest work. Okay, a deal's a deal. You guys agree with the lawyer that Bernice is unarrested, and free to resume her normal activities. He tells me you've agreed, in writing, Bernice will tell you where the slimy salvation is."

"Look, Mr. Witt, don't make it hard. Turn yourself in, it'll go easier on you and her."

"Do they still teach you guys to say that? I don't think I've committed a crime. Thank you for your help with the heavies, now please back away from the phone.

"Bernice, is he out of ear shot?"

She pressed the phone more tightly to her ear. "Yeah."

"I buried the Cuervo bottle next to the drain pipe under my trailer. The lawyer will hopefully keep you from being drugged. Keep 'em dancing for a couple weeks if you can."

"Sure. The young guy reeks of stud, should be pleasant."

Bernice hung up, smiling, and turned to the agents. "I'm going to go talk to the TV crew now. If you stop me I'll scream—thin walls, they'll hear me fine. Don't worry, I'm just going to praise you for collaring the four guys. If the phone rings it'll be my lawyer. Just ask him to hang on a minute till I get back in."

Frank Witt Dossier, FBI excerpt: On day fifteen of the investigation Mr. Witt's trailer and its contents were deconstructed into small pieces. When nothing was found, the ground underneath was excavated to a depth of five feet. A full bottle was discovered next to the drain pipe, but was revealed to contain only alcohol.

Four months later, Bernice was briefing her bartender and wait staff when the bar phone rang. The bartender made a move for the phone, but Bernice waved him off.

"Bernices. "Are you just as nicely packed as ever?"

"You son of a bitch! Abandoning me like that!"

"I hear the diner cash register wore out."

"Yeah, we've been full ever since the arrest, mob groupies and weirdos, and they pay, not like you."

"Sweetie, listen. The Feds will have this line tapped, so I'm not going to tell them anything they don't already know. Did you ever get it on with the young stud?"

"Nah, he was too married. You owe me a shot of the good stuff."

"Something else I'm going to have to welsh on. They'll pinch me if I try and see you, so we'll have to have phone sex." Frankie cleared his throat.

"I thought it out, Bernice. You were right. Giving away the tonic would have not only amputated my future income, it would've created competition. I drank it all. It's done—things—to me, mostly good, some not."

"You okay, you liar?"

"Yeah, thanks. I've got to finish under their trace time, so listen up. I found a corporate protector that uses my flesh and fluids for research and new products. I'm sort of a commercial Jesus, a golden goose providing the company with heaps of money. They also sell bits of me to the government, which keeps the feds less unhappy."

"So you guzzled down my shot."

"Yeah, sorry. But look under the rubber mat for serving drinks. There's an envelope for you."

"Wait a sec...Damn, Frankie, that's really my account?"

"It's twenty percent, like we said. Deposits every month from an offshore account." His voice changed, "and if you Feds dick with it I'll cut off your supply of me." His voice softened, "I miss you sweetie, but some of the weirdos take your picture for me, so I can see you're doing okay."

"Frankie?"

"I know."

Frank Witt Dossier, Joint Task Force excerpt: Bernice Sanders had been kept under tight surveillance for seventeen months when she eluded operatives and disappeared for two weeks. She returned with a deep total body tan and no explanation to friends, staff or federal informers as to where she had been. No trace of the elixir has thus far been found.

Uberism

By

Lance Hyden

The loud beeping sound from Isaac St. Martin's phone breaks his concentration from reading his book, "Irrational Fears," while sitting in his car. The beep every Uber driver loves to hear. It means financial gain; somebody's requested a ride! Isaac always finds a good place to park while waiting for his next passenger. Sometimes he naps, other times he listens to music or sports talk radio, occasionally plays candy crush, but this time he reads.

Isaac starts the engine and begins his trek to pick up the next client. He hopes that his next pick-up is a hot chick that will offer herself up to him. Of course that never happens, instead it will be one of the following; some drunk person trying to be responsible, or a Chinese college student majoring in finance, or even a stuck-up bitch that's clearly above everyone, or maybe an older couple that got a babysitter for the first time in 6 months. How about someone going to or coming from work? It could be a group of young guys hitting the town stinking of five different fragrances of "Axe" body spray, or someone that should have used Uber a few months ago instead of getting a DUI. What wonderful surprise will this pickup bring? This ride request takes Isaac to a nearby sports bar. The name of the passenger reads Jack, so Isaac shrugs his shoulder in disappointment. A man approaches the car and his walk reveals that he's had too much of Grandpa's cough syrup. Jack's wearing an Arizona State University shirt and doesn't look very happy with the outcome of the game.

"You my Uber driver?" he shouts through the window. Isaac, with an irritated look, asks for his name for verification because picking up the wrong rider can be a big hassle.

"Jack Carter," he responds with a slight slur in his speech.

"Then I'm your driver," Isaac confirms and the man opens the front passenger door and gets in. Isaac knows that when a rider chooses the front seat that signifies they're a seasoned... "Uberer? Uberist?" I guess there'll be a new term in Webster's Dictionary soon.

Isaac's first thought about picking up drunks is, like most Uber drivers, *I hope they don't puke in my car!* Jack's borderline one of these people. Isaac selects start trip and touches the navigate button to discover Jack's destination. This trip's end is only 3 miles away and Isaac's just fine with that. The shorter the ride, the less chance he'll yak in his car.

"Fucking Sun Devils lost to that shitty school in Northern Mexico. They cost me $20!" Jack rants as Isaac just nods and smoothly takes off his Arizona Wildcats baseball cap before Jack notices.

The drunken rant continues without pause between sentences. It's a superb filibuster performance with profanity, stats, and name calling. Isaac remains silent with a slight grin on his face. They reach the drop off point and Jack, now in tears, digs into his pocket to give Isaac $5.

Passengers aren't required to tip, but Isaac strongly disagrees, so he takes it.

"Thank you for getting me home safely and listening to me bitch," Jack says still weeping as he closes the door and walks away still muttering obscenities.

Five minutes into his book and Isaac receives a ding. A college football Saturday can make for a busy night and this request is two minutes away. The name reads Isabella and a slight rush of excitement tingles through Isaac's body. Women are his favorite to pick up. Although, this doesn't mean she won't be attached to some douche bag.

Isaac pulls up to the front of The Devil's Lair sports bar in Tempe and nobody's waiting outside. He usually waits a few minutes before calling or texting the passenger that he's there. After three minutes of waiting a gorgeous woman approaches the vehicle. She's alone, appears to be sober, and leans into the passenger window.

"Are you Isaac?" she asks to confirm her ride.

"Yes, I am," Isaac replies with a shaky voice. He's truly captured by her beauty. She sits in the back and Isaac gives a look of disappointment. She's wearing shorts and now his view of those sexy stems will be blocked for the entire trip. The good news, however, is that this trip's 15 miles away so he'll have her company for about 20 minutes. This trip was Isaac's 900th Uber journey, and by far his best one. They talked the entire time and he learned so much about Isabella Samantha Montgomery. The trip concluded at her beautiful and massive home at Indian School Manor. This was the first trip in which Isaac was truly sad for it to end, hopeful for that Uber driver fantasy- an invitation inside. Isabella gives him $20, says thank you, and walks away. Isaac drives off... alone.

It's been a very lucrative night and Isaac's exhausted. This will be his final trip for the night. The clock reads 2:36 a.m. and this will either be another drunk or someone getting off work.

Isaac pulls up to a dingy looking bar in a shady part of town. In the window a sign reads "Arizona's Home for Packer Fans." This, no doubt, is going to be a drunken redneck probably wearing a faded #4 Brett Favre Green Bay Packers jersey. He checks the name and it reads Ben. After several minutes Isaac grabs his phone and texts the rider; *I'm out front waiting. Thank you. Uber driver.* There's no response and he's getting upset and just wants to go home. He decides to give the Hick one more chance and dials his number.

"Uh, whb tis?" answers Ben with an extremely slurred voice. Isaac has a lot of experience understanding intoxicated people.

"It's your Uber driver. I'm outside waiting for over five minutes, I'm about to take off," Isaac says with anger in his voice.

"Okah, Mm wa ou," Ben replies then leaves his phone on and Isaac hears three minutes of dialog between two drunken idiots and has reached his highest level of irritation. Finally, he stumbles out of the bar, except he's not wearing a #4 Favre Green Bay jersey. It's much worse... a #9 Romo Dallas Cowboy jersey.

"Tay m hime!" Ben commands as he opens the door and falls into the backseat. Isaac looks at him in the rearview mirror and instantly hates this trailer park white trash. He's stinking up his car with the combination of cigarettes and cheap beer. Isaac clicks begin trip and no destination was entered.

"Hey bro, I need a destination, you didn't enter one," Isaac tells Ben and there isn't a reply. He looks into the backseat to discover Ben is passed out. Isaac reaches back and shakes his leg to wake him.

"Wha fuck mah?" the man yells out. Isaac knows he's in for a very annoying trip and is regretting his decision to take one more ride. Ben passes out again and Isaac decides to just drive away.

He stops the car down a dark unlit street nearby a trailer park that he thinks would be this fuckhead's home. Isaac gets out of the car, opens the backdoor, and drags his intoxicated passenger out by the legs then drops him onto the dirt road.

"You're home asshole!" Isaac shouts and is fuming with anger. Ben just lies there, out cold. He closes the backdoor, kicks him in the ribs several times, and gets back into the car. Isaac believes nobody will ever find out and this drunken asshole won't remember shit. He drives to the trailer park and selects complete trip. This would reflect on Isaac's trip history that's where Ben asked to be dropped off, and at 3:26 a.m., nobody's around to notice.

"Ubering" on Sunday morning during football season is always good for a few bucks. Most requests are people going to the sports bar to watch NFL games, or the hung over crowd wanting to retrieve their stranded vehicles from the previous night of drinking. However, the Sunday morning request that Isaac enjoys the most is what he calls "the ride of shame." Uber has single handedly destroyed the walk of shame. No more watching these one night stand beauties walking back to their dorm rooms, parent's house, or homes. Now just a couple of buttons on their phones and they can ride right past those peering judgmental eyes of strangers.

After a few rides Isaac's about to take the rest of the day off to enjoy his Sunday. He accepts one more chime and heads off to the pick-up location. The address looks really familiar and he gets the beginning of an erection as he figures out whose address this is. He's going to see Isabella Samantha Montgomery again!

He pulls into her driveway as if he's been there 100 times before. She's standing there already waiting and Isaac feels like he's picking her up for a date. He gets out of the car and opens the backdoor for her, something he's never done for any other passengers.

"So you don't want me to sit up front next to you?" she asks with a smile. He quickly shuts the backdoor and opens the front passenger door.

"I'm sorry. I just thought because last time you sat in the back,"he says embarrassingly as she climbs into the front seat.

"Well last time I didn't know you. Now you're my Uberman." She flirts. Isaac is over the moon with joy. His erection is now complete and he's trying to hide it. Isabella notices it and has a grin on her face as he walks around the car to get back in.

"When I saw the name Isaac on my Uber request I

was hoping it was you," she confesses and Isaac's face just turns bright red and he has a huge smile on his face.

"After I recognized this address and realized who I was picking up, I got so excited," Isaac admits.

"Yeah, I can tell," she says with a smile looking at his erection and Isaac's face turns another shade brighter and he goes silent as he begins the trip.

They arrive at Isabella's destination at the Indian Springs Mall. He would love to spend the whole day at the mall with her. Isaac always gauges the hotness of a woman one way, whether or not he would "hold her hand in the mall." If given the opportunity, he wouldn't let her hand go. She leans over and gives Isaac a kiss on the cheek and a $10 tip.   Isaac has turned off his Uber application and finds a quiet parking spot in the shopping mall's covered parking structure. He's done "Ubering" for the day, but there's one last thing he has to do before going home...unzip his pants and think about Isabella.

October was financially huge for Isaac and the last day of the month should be filled with interesting rides since it's Halloween. He knows there's the chance of annoying drunken ghouls, but on the positive side, his favorite costume women dressed as slutty...whatever. The clock in his freshly cleaned and fully gassed up 2013 Toyota Prius reads 4:52 p.m. He clicks the "go online" button on his Uber app and within a few seconds he's already got a request. Isaac slows down as the traffic signal turns yellow and then feels a sudden jolt from a vehicle rear-ending him. Isaac exits the car uninjured but pissed off and walks very quickly and ominously towards the car behind him. By the time he reaches the driver side window he is screaming like a madman. Behind the wheel is an extremely frightened 74 year old woman, but he doesn't stop.

"Watch where the fuck you are going. Were you texting, putting on makeup, or was it because you're so fucking old?" Isaac rants. The poor old lady has locked her door and won't come out of her car with this huge angry "Hulk" outside. A younger man that was walking by and witnessed the minor accident comes over to aid the old lady.

"Hey bro chill out, neither car has any damage and it was an innocent mistake." He tries to calm Isaac down from his frantic state by pointing out that both vehicles have no damage. Isaac turns towards him and looks as though he is going to pummel the guy to pieces. The man prepares to defend himself but Isaac immediately comes to his senses and stops his tirade.

After a few minutes the young mediator negotiates that no police or exchange of info is necessary and the trio conclude their discussion. Then they head off in their own directions. Isaac drives away but is still upset because he's lost a ride request.

Several rides later, Isaac has calmed down and forgotten about the fender bender with the white haired raisin. His phone has been going off with constant beeps for rides and almost every rider has been in costume for some sort of party or bar. Halloween on a Saturday night is going to be very lucrative and fun. He's just dropped off a Storm Trooper and a Jedi Knight going to a house party with a Star Wars theme. He clicks the "earnings" button and has made over $100.00 in just two hours. A great start to the night.

Isaac pulls over into a McDonald's parking lot to use the restroom and just as he enters the restaurant there's a ride request. Normally he would still use the restroom and then leave for the pick-up, but not this time. The name on this request reads… Isabella.

He arrives at Isabella's home in what seems like record time and is full of anticipation to see what sexy costume she'll be wearing. After a few minutes Isabella exits the house and is wearing a sultry devil's costume, and it doesn't matter that he's seen this "original" costume about 20 times tonight, because this one trumps them all.

Just as Isaac gets out of the car to open the door for the woman in red his huge grin immediately is erased as he sees a ripped Spartan warrior also exit from her home. He thinks how could she hide this information? She's never mentioned a boyfriend or husband.

"Hi Isaac, so glad I got you again. I'm starting to think you're stalking me," She says jokingly. Isaac isn't amused and just stares at this asshole that has ruined his fantasy of Isabella falling in love, marrying, and having five children with him. Isaac opens the backdoor for them, doesn't say a word, and gets back behind the wheel.

"Hey buddy, I'm Preston, Isabella's boyfriend. She tells me you've given her a few rides before. Probably not the kind of rides you're hoping for though," Preston says laughing. "Why don't you tell him how we met babe? I drive part-time for Uber and picked her up one day. Sorry! Beat you to her." He continues his taunt as Isaac begins the trip.

"Don't be a jerk Preston. Sorry Isaac, he's already

drunk," Isabella says, already knowing she's pissed off Isaac by withholding information about her love life. Isaac glares at him in the rearview mirror. Preston notices and gives him an evil like grin.

"Eyes on the road, or maybe you found someone better to look at. Fag!" Preston comments to try and antagonize Isaac.

Isaac remains quiet as he pulls up to their destination, The Devil's Lair, obviously Isabella's favorite watering hole and she's dressed appropriate for this night. Preston gets out of the car and immediately finds some other meathead, Spartan buddies that proceed to greet each other with masculine homoerotic chest bumps. Isabella remains in the car to talk to Isaac.

"Are you mad at me? I'm sorry I never told you about Preston. I was having such a good time talking to you that I completely forgot about him. We never have conversations like ours. Still friends?" Isabella pleads as he stares at her in the rearview mirror.

"Yeah, we're still friends but get rid of that idiot. You're too good for him," Isaac replies, and she gives him a hug, hands him $10, and then exits the car. He watches her walk into the congregation of steroidal Greek God wannabes. Isaac's not delusional, he knows his fantasy will never happen, but he also knows that piece of shit shouldn't be with her.

The night is coming to an end as the dashboard clock reads 1:37 a.m. He's had a great night with total earnings over $200. He's exhausted and wants to call it a night, but realizes that he's only a mile away from The Devil's Lair.

The parking lot is full of costumed people walking to their cars, taking cabs, or other Uber rides. No sign of Isabella or her Beast. A ride request comes in and the name says Jacob, he denies the request hoping the next one will be her.

Finally, after five rejected requests the name of his dreams appears. She's still here and most likely King Leonidas is too. Several minutes go by and Isabella exits the club with Preston following her. They appear to be arguing and Isaac gets out of the car to open the door, but mostly to make sure Isabella is safe. She jumps right into the back and Isaac shuts the door before Preston could get in.

"Open the door tough guy. Sorry, but I'm going to get to tap that hot ass while you go home and jack-off thinking about it," Preston says with an antagonizing tone, but Isaac doesn't take the bait and walks away. Preston opens the door and gets in. The two continue their argument as Isaac starts the car and drives off.

"Next time you make out with a chick on the dance floor, make sure your girlfriend isn't there asshole. First stop is Preston's house to drop him off because he won't be coming home with me," Isabella instructs Isaac. He looks in rearview mirror at Preston and gives him a cynical smile. Preston just flips him off.

They arrive at Preston's house and after pleading for Isabella to stay over and her saying no, Preston gets out and goes into his house. Isaac leaves to take Isabella home. They begin to talk about the night's events and what led to their fight.

"He had the nerve to fucking kiss some skank in

front of me, then try and invite her back with us like I would be okay with it. What a dirt bag," Isabella rants and Isaac just nods as she goes on about him all the way home. He pulls up to the front of her house.

"I should just let you come in and fuck me, see how he likes it. He's already texted me 10 times and called three more since our ride here. He just needs to go away or die, I'm done with him." She gets out of the car and says good night to Isaac. No tip, hug, or kiss this time.

"I guess she wasn't serious about me fucking her," he mutters to himself. He watches her go in to make sure she's okay and then he drives off.

A week goes by and Isaac has had over 80 rides earning over $1,000. Unfortunately, not a single rider was Isabella. He's covered areas she might be, drove past her house a few times a day, and hasn't heard from her since Halloween night. After several trips today he decides to do a quick drive by her house but before he arrives a ride request comes in and the name reads... Isabella.

Isaac pulls up to that familiar driveway and there stands his dream girl. Isabella jumps into the front seat and Isaac is very happy to see her, but she's not her normal happy self.

"Hey Isabella, what's wrong?" Isaac asks with genuine concern as he begins the trip. She takes a deep breath and sighs.

"How do you know me so well? I guess you didn't hear. Preston was found dead in his home. He was murdered Halloween night, sometime after you dropped me off. I got a text from him before I went to bed and the next day he was found dead by his brother," she explains. Isaac isn't terribly upset about it. In fact, a part of him thinks this presents an opening.

"I'm sorry. Anything I can do to help?" Isaac asks with intent to impress and win her affection.

"Actually, yes, take me back home. I was going to meet some friends and I'm not up for it. Perhaps you can stay and hangout with me?" she asks. Isaac instantly gets this rush over his body. He replies yes without hesitation and immediately turns the car around.

They enter her beautiful home and she tells Isaac to have a seat on the couch while she goes and fixes some drinks. Isaac walks over to the couch and remembers the advice that he read in a story from the book he's reading suggesting that guys should sit in the middle of the couch. That way the girl will have to sit right next to them. What a great opportunity to try this theory out.

Isabella returns with two glasses of red wine and she immediately sits right next to him. They take some sips and Isabella puts her hand on his leg. Isaac has a hard-on within seconds and takes more sips of the wine out of embarrassment.

"Oh, I've seen that before. Let me take care of that." Isabella teases as she puts her hand on his erection. Isaac is nearly ready to explode with excitement, but after a few seconds he no longer feels her hand rubbing his boner. In fact, he can't feel anything or even move a muscle.

"My dear Isaac, I'm not really sad about Preston dying. Truth is, I actually killed him. I'm going to tell the police that you've been stalking me and killed Preston out of jealousy. You picked me up today and started creeping me out. I requested for you to take me back home and that's when you forced your way in to rape me," Isabella explains. Isaac has a look of terror on his face as he realizes he's been drugged. She rips her dress off and mounts him putting his hard cock inside of her. She thrusts herself violently up and down on him until he ejaculates and there's no way to stop her. After he finishes she throws herself backwards onto her glass table shattering it.

"I'm sure you're confused. I've been targeted you since the first ride. I placed a tracker in your car so I would always be near to request a ride. Your ride history will look like you were stalking me. Your eyes are saying 'Why?' to me right now. Well, my father left me the Friendly Taxi Company when he passed, and because of Uber, my business is going under and I'm losing everything. Uber is too big to take down so I've decided I'm going to kill as many Uber drivers as I can, starting with you and Preston," she explains as she slowly gets up full of cuts. Isabella grabs a sharp piece of broken glass and puts it to Isaac's throat.

"The Police have a name for Uber drivers that stalk their passengers; they call it 'Uberism.' Good-bye my Uberman," Isabella says as she takes the shard glass and slits his throat. The last thought that enters his mind as blood squirts out from his neck is, "My fantasy came true... I think."

Imaginary Friend
By
Sarah Doebereiner

"I can't do this. Let's go home," Hannah suggested.

She shied away from an empty bed located horizontally against the wall of the otherwise bare room. After a moment of thought, she plopped down on the chrome floor and pulled one knee to her chest. Then she wrapped an arm around that knee to keep it from trembling. When Hannah first arrived, they brought her a warm blanket in exchange for everything else in her possession. Her ID, duffel, and even shoes retained their freedom somewhere beyond a locked door at the end of the tapered hallway.

"Shh. Don't talk like that. We need to be here," Penelope answered.

Hannah suffered from "Chimerism," the recurrent delusion that she and Penelope were completely individual people who had somehow become conjoined from the shoulder to the hip. The girls had two legs, two arms, and two heads. Each girl had control over half of the body. At first, walking had proven a challenge because when Hannah stepped forward on Penelope's side, the sensation more resembled a numb, glob of a stump than a foot. Now, the two moved in perfect sync. Penelope's thin, blonde hair fell across Hannah's face and tickled it until the skin on her nose wrinkled.

"I'll take my pills," Hannah vowed.

Heat from the vents caused the metal floor to creak. Soft, smooth drywall cushioned the walls behind them. Psych rooms always nestled on the interior of the complex to avoid any potential damage to the exterior of the building. Apart from a small window in the door for observation, the women were completely cut off from the rest of the world. The whitewashed nature of the space frightened Hannah. She felt as though they might get swallowed by its colorless static. She stared at the wall opposite where they sat, and wished for a view of the sky.

"As far as I know you never take it, Hannah. I'm sorry if that sounds harsh, it's just I wouldn't be there to know if you took it," Penelope scolded.

Hannah interlaced their fingers. She stroked the inside of Penelope's wrist with her thumb. The skin tingled under her touch. Warmth from her body flooded into the spot. Penelope twitched. She told herself it was the chill from the floor seeping into their butt and legs.

"I do, until I can't stand it anymore. I miss you. I miss you so much it burns my chest and makes it hard to breathe. My stomach gets flighty until I feel like throwing up, or I get stuck in the bathroom with anxiety driven diarrhea. At night, I look at your hand and cry because when I touch it, it's my hand," Hannah explained.

The skin on Hannah's cheeks pinked. She rubbed her foot against Penelope's foot. The motion calmed her nerves. Penelope raised her arm to sift her fingertips through Hannah's hair. Hannah leaned towards the touch, but Penelope let her hand fall short. Both women frowned.

"I can't comfort you. If I do, then you won't take me seriously. I can't hold you and tell you it will all be okay. Hearing that from me will make it worse," Penelope said.

"You don't know what it's like to suddenly be alone," Hannah lamented.

"For me, it's like falling asleep. I know time has passed, but I have no concept of how much," Penelope answered.

Hannah leaned backwards on the wall. The position put strain on their necks until Penelope was forced to join her. She angled her face in Penelope's direction. When she inhaled, the scent of rose petal perfume filled the air. Hannah held the breath for a moment to savor the aroma.

"I hate the thought of you like that, Penelope, just floating in nothingness."

"Yea," Penelope answered.

She couldn't lie; Hannah would know if she tried. Their heartbeat quickened. The thready pulse worked its way through Penelope and across to Hannah's side. Penelope tilted her face downwards. At home, she decided to remain as distant as possible to make it easier for Hannah to say goodbye, but she couldn't burry her own fear deep enough that her companion didn't perceive it. They were the same person after all. Penelope shifted her head until her lips brushed against the edge of Hannah's jaw.

"It's not good enough. I can't see you or talk to you. It's like you're dead," Hannah explained. Moisture gathered in the corners of her eyes.

"Listen, Love, I can't die. I'm not really here. Somewhere deep inside you must already know that, or else I wouldn't be able to think it. Chimerism - I'm just a phantom notion," Penelope asserted.

"You might as well ask me to cut a chunk out of myself," Hannah argued.

"Don't say that," Penelope snapped. She swatted Hannah's knee with a flat palm.

"I'll bash my head into this bed since it's bolted to the ground. Then, you can have the body, and I'll sleep the dreamless sleep," Hannah added.

"Hannah!"

"How is it different? How would that be any different?" Hannah asked.

"It just is. You're the real us," Penelope reminded her.

"Do you love me, Penelope?"

Tears erupted from Hannah's eyes. The flush in her face spread down to her neck. Tremors shook her lips. The side of their foreheads touched. From that distance, each woman could feel the breath from the other mingle with their own. Short sobs from Hannah shook their body.

"I love you. Of course I do; forever and ever and ever. That's why I want you to get well. I want you to be happy," Penelope affirmed.

"I'm happiest when we're together. Why is that wrong? I don't need to get fixed. Everyone has to get fixed and be ordinary and unhappy. I don't want to," Hannah pleaded.

"Yes, you do. I make it harder for you to interact

with real people; harder to keep a job. I'm not good for you, Baby," Penelope responded.

Hannah wicked moisture from her eyes onto their faded t-shirt. Wetness of the spot spread to Penelope's side. She tried to remind herself that goodbyes were always hard. Just because something felt right, didn't make it right. Hannah tugged her long, black hair in between her fingers until a piece ripped free of her skull. Penelope watched the discarded strands fall to the floor.

"I want you. We-," Hannah spoke. Though her voice was little more than a whisper the proximity if their heads let the words sound firmly in Penelope's ear.

"No," Penelope interrupted, "we agreed I wouldn't let you back out. It takes weeks for the medication to work. I won't vanish just because you take it once or twice. We'll work through it little by little."

"I'll always want you with me," Hannah argued.

"I want that to," Penelope sighed.

"You're real to me. Can't that be enough?" Hannah asked.

"It's not, Hannah." Penelope shook her head.

"You could be an extra-terrestrial parasite attached to my brain stem. Did you ever consider that? Remember that documentary on the Sci-Fi channel?" Hannah reasoned.

"Oh yea?" Penelope chuckled. "Maybe, I'm real and you're my hallucination. I just don't know it because the only time I'm with you is when I go off my meds."

"Yah think?" Hannah responded. Her eyes widened into vast, round saucers. A glimmer of fear shone in them.

Penelope squeezed their torso with enough strength to force the air out of their lungs.

"I was only kidding, Sweetie. One problem at a time, eh?" Penelope suggested.

Hannah stared through a small window in the door. Outside, a full-figured nurse doing rounds peeked in to make sure Hannah remained placid. She waved in the girl's direction.   The on-call staff had never seen "isolation sickness" present as Chimerism. Penelope thought curious excitement in the face of the girls' struggle was less than ethical.   This was the third time in as many years Hannah faced extended commitment. Penelope glared at the woman with scornful eyes until she wandered away. She crossed her leg under Hannah's and encircled their belly with her arm.

"Hannah?"

"Yes, Penelope."

"You aren't going to take the pills, are you?" Penelope asked.

"I will because you asked me to, but I probably won't when there is no one to force me," Hannah admitted. She glanced towards Penelope. Her jaw set into a tight line.

"You're hopelessly romantic," Penelope accused. A smile broke across her lips before she could squash it. A few moments of silence lingered between them.

"Hey, Hannah?"

"Yea?"

"I'm glad," Penelope confessed.

Killer Heels with a Side of Refitism

By
Tracey Chapman

Her face reflected in the red-patented leather stilettos, the wide maddening smile lit up her face. The flecks of blood were drying on the seven-inch stem as she displayed them nonchalantly with her growing collection. She lay down drifting peacefully off to sleep.

The early morning rays streamed through the trees. The lifeless body glistened with the drops of the early morning dew, and the gouged eye sockets were dark empty shells. Melissa Evans stared longingly out of her window. The commotion happening on the lower lawn below was intriguing. Pine Trees Sanatorium had been her home now for five years, her on off schizophrenic episodes detaching her from reality.

"Morning Lissie, breakfast time." Chirpy Morgan, as she was known, seemed to float in, deposit the tray, and float back out with all the joy in the world.

"What's happening out there?" Melissa's gaze never left the window.

"Come on Lissie, it's nothing for you to worry about. I've left your tablets here for you too."

Melissa turned, watching the scuffed up white sanatorium compulsory plimsolls disappear from view.

Melissa moved her breakfast round and round her plate. She opened the music box on her bedside table and peeled back the lining. A small pile of blue tablets covered the bottom. She took the next offering and added them to the box. The small ballerina twirled and twinkled, lowering as the lid closed shut. The blue flashing lights reflecting off the whitewashed walls captivated Melissa back towards the window.

The intensity was now growing on the lower lawn as an ambulance and police cars encompassed the gravel drive up to the house. The singular black body bag emerged from the tree line and a surge of excitement flowed through Melissa's body.

Counselling sessions were compulsory. Group therapy was supposed to bring benefits, but more often than not, Melissa would dream, distancing herself from the group and float off on a wave of silence. The unmistakable noise echoed in Melissa's ears. It was coming down the well-polished linoleum floor clicking, clacking in time. Melissa sat bolt upright in her chair, the droning voice of the counsellor fading into the background.

Melissa rose from her seat, and in her trance like state, walked straight through the counselling circle edging closer to the doo. Excitement building inside her, she peered through the glass; the black shiny leather caught her vision.

"Melissa, Melissa, will you be joining us at some point today?"

The shrill sound of the counsellor's voice forced Melissa to turn for a second, and on looking back through the glass the clicking, clacking was vanishing from view down the corridor.

"Oh Detective, have you time for a cuppa?" Chirpy Morgan was finishing off her usual tea round as they both nearly collided head on.

"Sorry I, I"

"Detective Rodgers, there you are. Shall we proceed to my office? Morgan please bring us some tea and biscuits."

Melissa still had the shiny black leather on her mind staring out of the double doors.

"Melissa you know if you joined in you really would benefit from it," the counsellor bent down removing the white plimsolls replacing them with an amazing pair of pale blue boots entwining laces stretching on for miles Melissa was mesmerized.

"Let's try again next week shall we?" Melissa had not even heard the response she just stared at her own blackened remnants of shoes five years' worth of hardship.

The screaming echoed down the corridor. Melissa, still fully clothed, woke from her bed with a start She felt dizzy, confused, she had not remembered coming back to her room last night. The screaming grew louder. Melissa peered from her room, it was old Mabel running, crying, still screaming. Melissa staggered down the corridor following the noise. A little gathering of patients had encircled around the kitchen doors.

The pale blue laces entwined cutting into the neck, the body calm and serene as though she lay there sleeping. Melissa knew those laces. She knelt down beside the body feeling the laces between her fingers, and a jolt of energy stunned her. The vivid image of the counsellor flashed through her mind, the shadowy figure pulling the laces tighter draining the life away, she could feel it, feel all the pain.

"Right, clear this lot away, secure this kitchen now."

Detective Rodgers looked down upon Melissa, the pale blue laces tightening around her wrists. She looked lost, detached.

"Miss, Miss, I just need to have a word with you," the gentle touch on the shoulder brought Melissa back she turned with such force bowling the detective over, tears streaming down her face.

"How did I get here? Where am I? Please someone help me, help me."

Chirpy Morgan appeared from the back of the kitchen, breakfast trolley in tow. She heard the sobbing from the end of the tables.

"Melissa, is that you?" Morgan edged down the side. Detective Rodgers was placing the handcuffs around Melissa's wrists.

"Wait Detective, please, she has schizophrenia; she's not in her right mind."

"I can't ignore this; she's here kneeling over the body and then assaulting me."

"Let me talk to her, calm her down in her room first, then come and find us. It's not like she's going anywhere."

Chirpy Morgan placed a comforting arm around Melissa.

"It's ok Melissa, we can make this all go away," she whispered closing the door shut behind them.

Morgan opened Melissa's closet the beautifully displayed shoe trophies made her heart skip a beat.

"You had everything, even though you were locked up in here. They still gave you everything, we're supposed to be sisters, and they always loved you more." Morgan caressed the pale blue boots, her latest accomplishment.

"Counsellors think they know everything, but they always have good taste in shoes. Now Lissie, did you take your tablets this morning?"

Morgan opened up the jewellery box, the small ballerina still twinkling and twirling away. She peeled back the blue lining and the small blue pills lay scattered.

"Oh Lissie, you have been a naughty girl. Let's get these down you and take away all that pain."

Morgan crushed the pills between her fingers and emptied them into her water bottle, shaking the powder away. Melissa still lay sobbing on the bed.

"Here we are Lissie, drink this it will make you feel better, take away that pain."

The cooling liquid flowed into Melissa's mouth and she looked up longingly into Morgan's eyes, a slight smile creasing her mouth.

"Night, night sister I love you."

The foaming blue liquid dribbled down Melissa's chin; she fitted, convulsing on the bed, it seemed an eternity but it was over in minutes. Morgan closed her sister's eyelids and kissed her forehead.

The knock on the door brought relief to Morgan. Soon it would all be over.

"Come on in Detective," the red stilettos fit like a glove as she stared longingly at them on her feet.

"At last I have something nice for me. See, sister I worked hard for these." Morgan hadn't noticed the Detective entering the room.

"Does she feel ready to talk now?"

"So sorry Detective, she seems to have fallen asleep must be that stress of what happened."

Detective Rodgers moved closer to Melissa, the blue liquid still stained her chin and covers. She could not make out the rise and fall of the chest, she bent down to feel the breath on her face.

"Are you sure she's sleeping?" Detective Rodgers felt for her gun holster unclipping the top with a flick of her thumb.

"Oh Detective, she's sound asleep." Morgan had bent down and removed the red stiletto. Feeling the patented leather in her grasp once more she raised the shoe above her head edging closer behind the Detective whispering softly to herself.

"Night, night Detective." the stem embedded into the Detective's shoulder sending the Detective reeling in agony to the floor. Morgan straddled the fallen foe.

"Detective, you should have left well alone. Me and my sister were fine. Look at what you made me have to do. Sorry but you know too much now," the blood dripped from the stem.

Rising again, Morgan could only hear the ringing in her ears as the bullet penetrated her chest. Lurching backwards with the force, the stiletto slipped from her grip. "It's over now," Detective Rodgers knelt retrieving the stiletto placing it across Morgan's chest.

The Dawn of Darkness
By
Charly Douglas

BE-ALLogique
BE-ALL You Can Be

"Have you ever wanted luxurious, creamy, dark skin?
Tired of spray tans that dot not go on even, streak or run?
Tired red of tanning beds or sunburns and the risk of skin cancer?

Well the good people at BE-ALLogique have developed a revolutionary
process that can be personalized to your exact desires. Imagine an
even, rich and permanent skin tone. Now imagine never having to
worry about skin cancer ever again.*
If you are ready for healthy, more vibrant skin
please contact a certified clinic in your area.

*BE-ALLogique has recently completed two years of clinical trials and
has received FDA approval for our patented PET process.
We accept all insurance carriers and work with them
to maximize coverage for this procedure.
Call today for more information!

Remember Goths? The pale kids shuffling down the road in 115 degree heat in black short sleeved t-shirts over black long sleeved shirts paired with extra-long, extra wide legged black pants. The bottoms of the pants were always tattered and frayed from being scraped across miles of grimy pavement. These kids never really bothered anyone. They just kept to themselves rolling in whatever real, imagined or parthenogenic sorrow that was overwhelming their soul. They never posed any real threat to the working class, much less our existence on this marble. Ah, the good ole days...

My name is Dr. Michael Haaland. I hold two PhDs in Human Psychology and Sociology. I believe that I am the last of my kind. This is my attempt to pass on the story of the end of our species on the planet Earth.

For anyone or anything who might find this, it is my version of what went wrong. I don't want anyone to look back on our civilization and wonder what happened. Where did an entire race, nay, planetary biome, go? It wasn't a comet, polar shift or even global climate change. It was us. We did this to ourselves. I always believed that humankind would kill itself but I could never decide on the when or how. Well, the when is now and I am going to explain the how.

The how boils down to vanity. I blame the insecure rich bitches and fame whores that were never happy with their self-image and the shallow men that forced their unrealistic, testosterone poisoned views on how females should look. The exploitation of women by men, the industry and themselves was ridiculous. The hardest I ever laughed was the day this woman walked through the lab in stripper shoes, twisted her ankle and knocked two teeth out. I swear there should have been some kind of driver's test to walk in hooker heels in public. They were a goddamned menace and safety hazard. I am sure they thought they looked sexy because that is what society told them, but they looked like broke-neck chickens trying to walk on hot coals. All of these things and more were the catalyst.

It started with body hair removal, lip plumpers, permanent make-up and Wonderbras, which quickly graduated to plastic surgery. I remember girls, GIRLS, in high school getting breast augmentation. To achieve a darker skin tone, pills were created to tan you from the inside out. The only problem was that they destroyed your liver and made you blind. Next, were the tanning beds that increased skin cancer despite claims to the contrary. Spray tans were safer but temporary, and they were notoriously uneven and produced the trademark Scottsdale Orange skin tone, which I believe, had its own Pantone color swatch right next to Jersey Burnt Orange and Gypsy Dark Amber. Geez, they sound like microbrews.

Where there is a market, there is a way… all hail capitalism. Enter BE-ALLogique…

BE-ALL was a private, for-profit company backed by Caden Warner, the angel investor behind the XXXTan-thin pills and the Hydroskin craze. This was a man who knew how to profit off of people's insecurities and since he was only a financier he could not be held liable for the devastating effects of these products. His lawyers were paid well to insure that nobody could touch him or his amassed wealth. When the shit hit the fan, he disappeared faster than Walter Palmer.

Gethin was an old Welsh name that meant dark-skinned and "Geths" were the new Goths. Instead of being pale, they were dark via a chemically enhanced tan. They were also known as "PETs" and that name came from the process that darkened their skin. The term "Gethinism" was originally coined to define this newly preferred look but soon became a description of the morphology and psychosis displayed by Geths.

Gethinism started in the U.S., in Scottsdale, Arizona to be precise. In 2011, in the back labs of BE-ALLogique, clinical trials for a new process called PET (pigment enrichment therapy) were initiated and made available to the public. Within two years the PET process had quickly spread to all industrialized countries in the world. If you can envision a cross between dyeing eggs and getting a full body tattoo then you would be pretty close to imagining the process.

Those who could afford it, paid to have themselves dipped into a clear chemical cocktail. The more dunks, the darker the skin. I'm not talking about orange. I am talking about shades of dark, silky chocolate. This was just the first phase of the process.

The second phase equated to being vacuum-sealed, but instead of plastic bags, it was a newly engineered type of neoprene. Before being dipped, a mold was taken of the individual's body and then a clam-shell suit was made of the material. The inner surface was imbedded with nano-needles and after dipping they were sealed in the suit for up to forty-five minutes per session. The pressure and the needles pushed the cocktail into the stratum basal layer of skin which hijacked the melanocytes and altered melanin production.

The process also had the added benefit, or side-effect (depending on your predisposition), of soaking into hair follicles and permanently dyeing your hair as well. If you didn't want your hair processed then that was a whole different procedure of a chemical pretreatment and a post-dip stripping while the rest of your body was in the clam shell. The whole process took hours. The irises of the eyes also darkened so colored contacts were prescribed, if wanted.

As with most pseudo-medical beauty treatments, this one was based off of real medical studies related to skin pigmentation and cancer. The odd thing was, that after three years, the treatment proved itself to be a 100% effective at preventing melanoma and the process received full FDA backing. Once that hit the news the medical insurance companies were lobbied to cover it. While Europe and South/Central America had adopted it almost immediately without any required government approval, the backing of the U.S. government gave Gethinism PET an official push to go global.

The same thing that made the PET process so effective in preventing skin cancer was also the cause for the rise in other complications. Many secondary illnesses were due to severe vitamin D deficiency because the UV rays couldn't penetrate the skin. One hundred percent of the Geths suffered from Seasonal Affective Disorder but the correlation wasn't discovered because the majority of them were on anti-depressants and vitamins. All of the related suicides went unrecorded as well. Medical issues that were swept under the rug included strokes, diabetic comas, dementia and schizophrenia. All were chocked up to heredity or lifestyle choices.

Early in 2017, other studies started surfacing. Miscarriages and birth defects were on the rise but there was no true correlation to Gethinism because it was happening in the non-Geth population as well. Excessive lifestyles were blamed once again as new designer drugs were hitting the streets every few months. Within two years, stillborn births and infertility in Geths were at 100% and statistics for non-Geths were rising sharply.

Why couldn't we stop it? Humans en masse are arrogant, ego-centric, and immortal-minded creatures. Why did this take seven years to surface? The early adopters were young, vain women who didn't want stretch marks and aging women trying to recapture a youthful appearance while everyone of childbearing age in the middle couldn't afford the treatment. BE-ALLogique and its investors kept things tightly wrapped as long as possible to protect their pockets. They didn't realize that Death didn't accept cash or credit, he wanted their corrupted, shattered souls.

You see water, the one thing above all else that keeps us alive and functioning, the one thing we would die without in 7 days, was what sealed our fate. Our one last scourge on Mother Earth and it only impacted humans. PET chemical spills and waste products invaded our ground water supply, made their way through our rivers, into the oceans and icecaps and were ingested by the aquatic life we ate. Again, their genome was just different enough for them to survive until we ate enough of them to poison ourselves. The non-Geths were dying of systemic failures, primarily liver and kidney failure.

What made us different from the other animals was our downfall. That small percentage of the human genome, the 1.2% that enables high functioning (some more than others) and critical problem solving, finally decided that we were too stupid to survive as a species. The body began to mutate after the chemical bath and poisonous ingestions. It shut down reproductive paths and aborted any attempt to propagate the species. By the time the most intelligent of us realized the implications, it was too late to stop it. There wasn't enough time to find a way to purify the water, much less find a way to stop, reverse or cure Gethinism. Sure the scientific community tried but most opted for a bullet in the end. We were all self-appointed gods who blasphemed the sacred significance of science.

Finally, a symptom unique to Gethinism emerged that couldn't be explained away or ignored. The prolonged lack of vitamin D combined with the stress from the ancillary issues caused the fascia to deteriorate which resulted in necrotic fasciitis. Over the next few months the Geths' bodies no longer recognized their largest organ and started to reject it. For those with fewer dunks, the skin initially bubbled in small localized patches. Others, who had been more liberal with their exposure, began to slough off their skin in swathing patches. The chemicals had also settled into their joints causing gnarled hands, hunched backs and difficulty walking.

When the skin reactions first started everyone thought it was an allergy to a new laundry detergent or a venereal disease gone wrong. A few work days missed here or there, some urgent care or free clinic visits, not much to worry most. Except that nobody got better over time and the numbers rose steadily.

The new Gethinism was dawning and with it mass panic, suicides and homicides… a new "Wellian" age of terror. Mankind had finally found a way to kill itself and there was no way to get off this ride. Between direct contact and the poisoning of the world's food and water supply by the PET waste products, everyone was sterile by the year 2020.

Those that had lesions that could be hidden continued to work and hid their secret for fear of being fired or worse, judged. Within a year businesses started shutting down because there weren't enough workers. Who cares if a coffee shop goes out of business but what about when it's the medical supply warehouse or the grocery stores?

It was terrifying to think that a zombie-like apocalypse was actually starting and comical the way the religious left was flailing prostrate because they predicted Armageddon was coming. Of course they predicted it every few years or so but, by the grace of God, they got it right this time.

A pandemic of this proportion had never been seen before in history. It overwhelmed medical facilities around the world. Between the hoarding influx of patients, the waning staff and lack of supplies, the medical facilities were abandoned.

Riots and looting arose from the financial collapse, suicides from hopelessness and homicides from fear. Quarantines and curfews became mandatory until law enforcement and peace keeping efforts were abandoned. Mass exodus from the cities began as the violence escalated and Maslow's hierarchy dwindled.

Maybe it was our higher collective consciousness that decided our evolution had exceeded its capacity for compassion and therefore accelerated de-evolution by self-genocide. We had destroyed the planet, were responsible for the extinction of 322 species in the last 500 years and ejected our garbage into space. Some thought that God was smiting us, but I didn't think so. If there really was a God he would have started from scratch centuries ago.

The last supply mission's contents were doubled to allow NASA time to figure out how to keep the resource route flowing. A basic shipment for four people at a three month supply, times two, could allow one person to survive up here well over 24 months if portioned properly. Between launch and arrival in 2019, Dr. Saeversson (botanist) had already overdosed and Dr. Rice (physicist), had slit his wrists. We still had plenty of reserves before it arrived but Colonel Keeto was small and easy to overpower. I smothered her while she slept the evening that the supplies arrived. I was going to make it home.

All radio transmissions stopped by the end 2020, and in March of 2021, I saw the mushroom clouds. I guess without maintenance and proper manning, some of the nuclear systems' fail safes were, well, failing. There was no way to tell if a button was pushed intentionally or if it was a failure at the silos, but something triggered a launch which triggered the counter launch.

Watching from up here, I have to admit that it was

beautiful… and debilitating. The only thing worse than the end of the world is being the only one left to watch it. Now that the other three are dead I will have to recalculate my air supply. Does it really matter now? I can't go home. I will continue to translate and record this message into as many languages that this system knows. I will send one set in a pod back to earth before I die, one into space and leave one onboard. I don't know if anyone or anything will find them or if they will be comprehended.

My name is Dr. Michael Haaland, it is the 13th of March 2021, and I believe that I am the last alive of my species. I went to the International Space Station in 2017 with the intention of breaking the record set by Gennady Padalka at 879 days in space. I succeeded. Be-ALL my ass.

ODDisms

Perfect, Bifurcated Unity
By
DJ Tyrer

I must admit to feeling apprehensive when I received an invitation from Brent to visit him at his ranch in Texas. I'd heard a rumour he'd started farming llamas and the only thing I knew about llamas, if you discounted the fact they're not the same thing as lamas, is that they spit. I didn't want to be spat at.

But, I couldn't really blow it off, so I let him know when I'd arrive. I made sure to pack a sou'wester, just in case.

It turned out it was actually an alpaca farm. It also turned out that alpacas are pretty much the same as llamas; I wish someone had told me before one spat in my face.

Brent was waiting for me on the porch of his ranch house dressed in an Andean poncho and a Stetson with a possum flopped upon his shoulders. A three-toed sloth hung from the front of the porch roof and a bald eagle sat on a perch beside the front door. I looked at the latter; I was fairly certain they were illegal to own. I didn't say anything.

He jumped down and gave me a hug. Brent had always been more demonstrative than I was comfortable with and he seemed particularly effusive today.

"Come inside," he said. "Dinner is prepared."

"I, ah, like what you've done with the place," I said

as I followed him inside. A large table was set with two places and a number of courses.

"It is a homage to the two Americas. North and South," he elaborated, doubtless noticing my eyebrow twitch upward, questioningly. "Be seated."

I sat down and he served us nachos as a starter.

"We have Argentinean beef and Canadian bacon," he said, gesturing to plates.

"Another homage?"

He nodded. "Plus, possum pie. Mm-mm, tasty!"

I refrained from pointing out that it seemed to be rather sick to be feasting on possum pie while your pet possum slouched about your shoulders nibbling at titbits of roast potato he offered it.

"Yes, all very tasty," I said, tucking into a lovely chunk of roast beef while carefully avoiding any pie that wasn't apple.

"Viva the Americas!" he toasted with a glass of Chilean wine. I echoed the toast.

"So," I asked after a while, "did you bring me down here just to fatten me up or was there some other reason?"

"Not at all," said Brent. "Although, can there be anything more American than eating well?"

"True."

"But, no, that wasn't my primary reason. Have you been following my blog?"

I had to admit that, no, I hadn't. I'd given up years before when he started comparing cats he thought looked like Hitler in a search for the Fuhrer reborn; I didn't condone the drowning of cats, whatever the reason. I had no idea what further nonsense had come to obsess him.

"Well, if you had," Brent said, sounding a little aggrieved, "you would know I've been the world's leading proponent of 'Ambi-Americanism.'"

"Ambi-what, sorry?"

"Ambi-Americanism."

"Which is?"

"The bringing together of the two Americas –"

"North and South?"

"Yes. Bringing them together into one unified whole in which two equal and distinct halves act together. It's why I created this place; it's my temple to that unity."

"And," I prompted, "you brought me here for, what? To convert me to your cause?"

"Perhaps, although I know you're most likely thinking it's nothing but eccentricity. But, mostly, I wanted you here as a witness."

"A witness? A witness to what?"

"A witness as I strike the first blow for Ambi-Americanism."

I didn't like the sound of that. It was like learning I'd been invited to observe his resolution of the Hitler-reincarnation conundrum. With Brent, you could never be entirely certain what he had planned. Still, I took solace in the fact he couldn't increase the speed at which the North American continent was ploughing southward. Or, was it South America ploughing northward? Either way, there was no way in which he could increase the speed and cause some terrible disaster and, beyond that, I couldn't conceive what form his mania could take, beyond the already-evident intermixing of fauna and foods from north and south of the equator.

"Follow me," he said, pushing his plate aside. The possum hopped down from his shoulders to nibble at the remnants of the pie containing one of its relatives. I suppressed the urge to gag at the thought as I stood to follow him.

We exited the ranch house and headed for a barn on the far side of the alpaca enclosure. As they looked at me with what I took to be beady eyes, I wished I'd fetched my sou'wester from the boot of my car.

Brent flung the barn doors open and strode inside with all the swagger of a banker. I followed after him, far less confidently.

"There you go," he said, pointing to a shadowy corner. "My triumph."

I followed the direction of his gesture, expecting to see some new South American animal that was to be the star-attraction of his Pan-American menagerie, but it wasn't. Instead, I saw two figures trussed up like the proverbial pig. I recognised one immediately; it was the President of the United States of America. Who wouldn't recognise him? There are, I'm sure, remote tribesmen with only the barest comprehension of the outside world who would recognise him.

"You've got the President tied up?" I groaned. Then, I pointed at the other person and asked, "And who's that? The President of Mexico?"

He laughed. "Don't be silly; it's the President of Venezuela."

114

"Venezuela?" I groaned again.

"Exactly. These two are the main impediments to bringing the two halves of the Americas together in perfect, bifurcated unity."

Which, I suppose, was true, but hardly welcome news.

"Did you know," he asked, straying off the point, "that the possum has a bifurcated penis? Two members working as one for the greater good of the possum species; the perfect metaphor for Ambi-Americanism."

I was sure I could have thought of better ones, but it was just then that we became aware of the *thromp* of rotor blades.

"Oh, no!" Brent exclaimed. "They've found me!"

"Surrender!" a loud-hailer-distorted voice called. "We have you surrounded! This is the Secret Service, with the FBI, Texas Rangers and Venezuelan Special Forces, and, I repeat, we have you surrounded: surrender, immediately!"

Brent turned to me with a broad grin.

"What are you smiling for? This is terrible, you fool!"

"But, don't you see?"

"See what?"

"I've achieved a success of a sort; a first step towards bringing the Americas closer together."

"What do you mean?"

"The USA, Venezuela – even Texas – all working together and all because I kidnapped these two idiots. A perfect first step!"

I rolled my eyes. My friend was a fool. Not an

absolute fool, for he'd managed to kidnap two heavily-guarded presidents, but a fool nonetheless.

I ran to the door and shouted, "I surrender! This has nothing to do with me!"

Brent sauntered after me with no sign of concern, calling, "I guess I surrender, too. You can have your presidents back." To me, he added, "I've had a chance to lecture them about Ambi-Americanism, and it's been a successful gesture, so I'm happy."

"I'm so glad one of us is," I muttered as the FBI, or possibly the Secret Service, took us into custody. I had a bad feeling we might be going to Gitmo.

I might've felt a twinge of sympathy for Brent, except he looked quite pleased with himself.

I just had to hope I could convince them I'd had nothing to do with any of it. I certainly wasn't pleased.

Poker Farce

By

Karen Robiscoe

"**D**eal," Cody says, in a commanding tone to the Duke. He's so excited to start the game of Blind Man's Bluff, he's drooling. His enthusiasm is contagious. His anxious fidgets riling the other assembled poker players to the point that the room's become a cacophony of twitching gamblers and howling card sharks, and for a moment, the Duke wishes the door in the kitchen had already been shut for the day when Cody arrived. Cody's too excitable by far, is what it is, and flicking cards toward the group assembled around the felted green table with random precision, Duke squashes his instinct to instantly retrieve them by scraping divots with his overly long nails into each released card's patterned back. His mark, and *his* party, and he damn well doesn't care what the other players think about it, either.

In seconds the players have their hands—as well as their attitudes about their hands—and Cody sniffs the air automatically, practically smelling the sweat break out on his buddy Trouble, so named due to his tendency to start fights with unsuspecting rollerbladers. Trouble has an unreasonable fear of rollerbladers, and quite possibly bad cards too. The Duke takes this under advisement as he licks, nibbles, and sticks the very best card he has to the crown of his head. The other players follow suit, affixing the cards to their brows and heads to mimic the Indian braves for which the poker game is named.

"I'm going first," the Duke says, grimacing a bit threateningly as he pushes chips toward the table's center. "My house—my rules. I bet two."

"I'll call your twooOOOOOoooo!" Snoop Dog sing-songs. "And raise it twooOOOoo, toooOOOoooo!"

"That's four to you, Cody."

"I'm out," Tiger decides, tossing his cards to the felt, face down. He demonstrates both a lack of breeding and poker etiquette by pushing away from the table, and scratching his balls with great gusto.

"Cody?" The Duke growls, irritated he can't join Tiger—his balls suddenly itch fearsomely, too—and put out to remind Mr. Raring-to-Go. "You want to play, Cody?"

"Do I!' Cody rejoins, so worked up he literally jumps from his chair to run circles around the poker table. "Do I! Do I, do I, do I, dooOOOoo!"

"Cody!" the group barks in stereo, but the excited fellow can't control himself. He *is* getting on in years, Duke thinks. Even in dog years Cody would be considered over-the-hill and Duke wonders if it's possible to be afflicted with hyperactivity *and* "Old Timers" simultaneously.

"Stop that this minute!" the Duke adds. The interruption is particularly upsetting; Duke's almost positive he has the highest card stuck to his brow. Snoop's the only one with a picture card, and it's just a green one, and throwing all social nicety to the wind, he does the unthinkable.

He leashes Cody, and leads the agitated golden retriever out to the yard.

A Vacation Fit for a King

By

Veronica Smith

Stanley Groves was an avid reader and Stephen King's number one fan. He'd read all of his books and was completely hooked. When his vacation time came around he decided to do a Stephen King book/movie binge-a-thon. He bought every book he didn't already have and rented every movie. His plan was to read the book and then watch the corresponding movie. He planned to spend most of his two weeks vacation doing this. He turned off his cell phone, stocked the fridge and locked his door.

Four days later he was eating breakfast at 4:30 in the afternoon and realized he'd hardly slept. His King addiction had confused his body so much he didn't even realize it was late afternoon and Eggos weren't just for breakfast anymore. He yawned and decided to sleep through the night before continuing on with the marathon. "I wonder if there is a Guinness World Record for this," he chuckled to himself as he set his alarm for 8:00 a.m. Almost as soon as his head hit the pillow he was out like a light.

He woke to a car honking right outside his window. He rolled over and covered his head with a pillow, ignoring the rude neighbor. The honking continued and as he sat straight up, he remembered the neighbor's driveway was on the other side of his house. There was only grass outside his bedroom. He crawled out of bed and cautiously peered out between the curtains. High beam headlights blinded him as the car honked again. "What the hell are you doing on my lawn?" he yelled. "I'll call the cops on you!" The headlights blinked out but the honking continued. Once his eyes adjusted to the darkness and the street lights reflected off the car, he stopped yelling. "What the hell?" he whispered to himself. The car looked to be a red 1958 Plymouth Fury. "No fucking way!" he swore. "I'm calling the cops right now!" he threatened the silhouette behind the wheel. "Go ahead you shitter!" the driver replied. Somehow he was heard inside the house perfectly fine. The car surged forward and Stanley dropped the curtains and backed up. The sound of the car crashing through the wall was as loud as the engine and, as the car crushed him, he heard laughter.

"Oh shit, what a nightmare!" he said out loud as he woke with a start. He was drenched in sweat and shaking. "If only I really had a 1958 Plymouth Fury," he laughed. He tried to get up and found he was tied to the bed. He looked around and saw a large shadow in the corner of the room. "What are you doing in my house?" he yelled. "I'll call the cops!" Suddenly he felt déjà vu. *Didn't he just yell that out already to someone else?* The shadow moved closer and, although he could see the shape was a woman, the glint of the steel blade of the axe she was holding stood out more. "I have money," he begged. "Hundreds in cash if you want it. Take it, it's yours." She moved closer to him and pulled the covers off of him. She positioned herself near the foot of the bed and he began to whimper. "Please, God, no." As she swung the axe downward towards his ankle, she said sweetly, "God, I love you."

"No!" he screamed into his pillow. But it wasn't a pillow. He found himself face down in the gutter like a drunk passed out in the street. The softness on his face was a pile of leaves that collected at the edge of the sewer. He got to his knees and realized that the leaves were wet and soaked through his pajamas. "Damn," he said. "It looks like I pissed myself." "Psst." came from somewhere nearby. He looked around to find the whisperer. "No, down here." He craned his neck to look into the sewer and, incredibly, saw a clown with bright red hair and a high white forehead. "Do you need help?" Stan asked him, "Are you stuck down there?" The clown laughed. "Of course not, silly," he giggled as he grabbed Stan's pajama collar. "We all float down here!" Stan screamed but couldn't pull loose of the grip that was pulling him closer. The smell was so rank he threw up, still trying to pull away. One final yank and he found himself falling through until he landed hard on his back.

Hard, but yet the ground was soft; carpeted even. "What the fuck?" he muttered, running his fingers through the plush gray carpeting. He looked around at the long hallway and face planted in the carpet. "No more," he whispered, "I can't take any more." "Come play with us." He jerked his head up at the voices speaking in unison. Twins. But of course it would be the twins. "No, no, no!" he closed his eyes and shook his head violently. "Not real!" he screamed. He passed out at the words, "Forever and ever…"

And woke up in his bed. "I need a fucking cup of coffee," he said as he got out of bed. As he walked past the window he stopped, half expecting to hear honking. He laughed at himself and almost kept going until he heard the scratching. Like fingernails on a chalkboard but they were on glass. With shaking hands he pulled open the curtains to see a small shape floating outside his window. Long dirty fingernails scratched at the glass in long slow arcs. Even though his house was a single story, the figure was at least five feet off the ground. "Let me in," said a soothing, hypnotic voice. "Open the window." Stan wanted to run away but he couldn't. Against his will his hands reached for the lock and unlatched the window. As he raised it up he felt, more than heard the swoosh, as the figure came inside and floated next to him. "I'm so hungry." "I have Eggos," Stan replied weakly, his will draining away. "Not Eggos . . ." He felt small hands grab his hair and pull his head back. Sharp pain in his neck broke the spell as he screamed and stumbled around the room. He tripped over his shoes and crashed to the floor.

His suit was ruined. He found himself on his hands and knees on the floor. Water and blood pooled all over the floor and debris was everywhere. Drenched and burned decorations hung in tatters from the ceiling. There were bodies lying on the floor and draped on the tables. He heard screaming people everywhere. "At least it's not me screaming this time," he said wryly. He looked in that direction and saw people pushing at a door. They were all in dresses and suits, much like himself. "Welcome to the party pal," he joked in his best Bruce Willis impression. He shakily got to his feet to see a young woman on the stage in front of him. She was in a party dress but it was impossible to tell the color as she was completely drenched in blood.

"Whose blood?" he asked himself, not really wanting to know the answer. He didn't realize he spoke out loud until she heard him and focused her gaze on him. He backed up, putting his hands out in a feeble attempt to block . . . something. Her eyes opened wider and a blast of pain, shock, and pure whiteness slammed into him. All he could hear was a beeping siren, echoing in his head as it exploded.

Beep. Beep. Beep.

His alarm clock blared in his ears, waking him slowly. He slammed a hand down on it to shut it up and looked at the time, 8:00 a.m. "Damn," he said as he ran his hand through his sweat drenched hair. "I bet I didn't get any damn sleep. No more straight through bingeing. I take breaks and sleep at night for the rest of the vacation." He shook his head and padded into the kitchen to put on a pot of coffee. Just as the pungent smell of urine hit him he slipped in the puddle and landed with a splash on his back. "Great," he said, the back of his head already aching from the impact. "I'm lying in a puddle of dog piss." He closed his eyes then said, "but I don't have a fucking dog!" As he opened his eyes, a runner of drool dripped into one of them, blurring his vision. But he still had one good eye and was able to see the foaming snout of a dirty Saint Bernard as its mouth opened and tore out his throat before he could even scream.

Hackism 101

By

Matt McGee

A silver Toyota SUV floated down the hill toward Padri's Ristorante at a speed the valets know well. The pace of an approaching customer differs from the average driver going to the movie theatre across the street or the local sushi bar. The two men in red jackets watched the truck slow to a stop, then moved into action.

Ramone, olive-skinned and the older of the two, swung to the driver's side door, while Parker swung open the passenger. "Good evening, welcome to Padri's." He held the door and watched a well-dressed woman in a high-cut dress smile, slide discretely out of the truck and slide away.

Then, Parker watches Ramone for the signal.

An empty right hand. This is Parker's green light to climb behind the wheel while Ramone returns to the valet stand. With nothing new in their tip box, Parker is free to dispense as much automotive justice as he sees fit.

There are three speed bumps leading to the rear parking lot, and Parker likes to think he's worn them out a little with the wheels of non-tippers. He leaves the Toyota's alarm off then jogs back to the valet stand. Ramone is perched on the stool, flipping through a glossy magazine.

"So remind me," Ramone says. "What's it like being twenty-two?"

"I can still comb all my hair and my knees don't hurt

when I run. Been a while for you, huh?"

"I can't remember what it was like having unwrinkled skin and pussy up to my armpits. The only thing I don't miss about being younger – eating dog shit food. I don't mind doing without a doctor visit or trip to the dentist once a year. But I *will not* eat junk food anymore. *That* I'll spend money on."

Parker leaned against an idle Nissan. They'd kept it out front because it looked pretty cool and the guy had tipped them $10. "You know how when you go into Jack in the Box and pay for your food, they give you your change and then they stuff that annoyingly long receipt in your hand? And you don't know what to do with it, but you don't want to throw it out just in case they screw up your order - or worse yet, lose all trace of your purchase."

Ramone flipped a page of the magazine. "Yeah, sure."

"You stick it in your pocket or fold it into your wallet until that one day a year when you're just carrying too much paper and finally you have to thin it out. So you pull out this Jack in the Box receipt from four months ago and say to yourself, 'why the hell did I hold onto this piece of crap?' And finally, faded from age and wear in your wallet, it makes it into a trash or recycling can."

"Got a few of those in my wallet now."

"Well, that's how I eat."

Ramone looked up.

"I can walk into almost any Jack in the Box parking lot and find a discarded receipt within seconds. I then go on my cell phone, do the survey real quick, then go inside and redeem the code for two free tacos. No money spent and the manager on duty gets a five-star rating to look good in front of his boss. It's win-win."

"Sounds like you're just being cheap."

"I call it 'Hackism.'"

Ramone nodded and smirked. "We have our share of cheap bastards around here."

"They may think they can skip out on tipping the valet, but the last person you want to life-hack is the king of hacking. How many guys have handed over their Jag keys without slipping us a couple bucks?"

"Too many."

"And they expect to get their car back without a severe pull in the steering."

"Why do they do that?"

"Man if there's one thing that drives me batty in life, it's the guys in their forties or fifties with a million in the bank yet they're still life-hacking thru everything like college freshman. Or the rich women with their $500 haircuts driving a hundred thousand dollar Tesla...because they think skipping the gas station is a life hack. Leave that to me, OK? I'm twenty-two. I'm supposed to be cutting corners until I find my place in the world."

"You bet."

Parker shifted his ass against the Nissan. "Problem is, during the last year this little lifestyle has dominated my time. Like, I haven't paid for a fountain drink at the corner gas station for almost a year."

"Which one?"

"The USA up on the corner," Parker pointed. "I haven't paid for anything but gas since that long, heartfelt talk I had with the cashier."

"You bone her?

"No, she's got two kids and a baby daddy in her house."

Ramone nodded. He flipped a page.

"Her kids," Parker went on, "they'd been begging for guitar lessons. And since I'd showed up with a gig bag in my backseat, I agreed to spend an afternoon giving her sons lessons on a bunch of secondhand equipment I own."

"Were they any good?"

"To be honest, they could've started a band. The one kid picked up chord structure as soon as I showed it to him. The other didn't just whack on the old snare and cymbal I brought. He did it with rhythm. Point is, ever since then, I haven't paid for a soda."

Parker finally looked over the podium to get a good look at Ramone's magazine, finding as expected, the naked torso of an airbrushed woman. He rounded the podium and raised a brow in approval. Then he reached under the podium for his own reading material, *A Christmas Carol*. Ramone saw the title.

"You do know it's the hottest part of the year."

Parker opened to his bookmarker. "That's what makes it good. It's like having something you're not supposed to have." He nodded at Ramone's magazine. "Like her."

"Her? Pfft. She ain't nothing. My girl puts her to shame. Where'd you get that old-lookin' book anyway?"

"No one's got more good, cheap books than the library. I can get an education for $20 a year just by going to the local library and picking up everything that looks interesting."

"Is that where all your tips go?"

"Money well spent. And it isn't much money. They're like fifty cents here, two bucks there."

"Another hack?"

"Hack. You know what I read about last week?"

Ramone's eyes were back in the magazine.

"I read about the secret underground history of Portland."

"You mean like Nirvana and Pearl Jam?"

Parker rolled his eyes. "No, that was Seattle. Portland used to be loaded with ships, and the ship owners couldn't always get enough men to come work on their boats. So they'd get them drunk. And when they were passed out they'd whisk them away."

"Where?"

"I'm getting to that. They'd whisk them away through a series of underground tunnels. These tunnels would pop out at the harbor, and they'd drag the drunk guys onto the boats. Once they had enough of them locked up, they'd set sail to Shanghai. Hence the term Shanghaied."

Ramone may have been talking to his magazine, but he said, "damn."

"There were life-hacks even back in the day."

"So you're saying I should be grateful I'm actually free to come and go from work."

"Yep."

The motor of a sports car sounded at the top of the hill. Without looking, both men slipped their reading material back under the podium. The whine of a big cat coming always meant business. This one was a bit of a surprise.

The powder blue car roared up, its orange racing stripe flashing in the light of the restaurant. Parker's eyes popped open.

"Holy shit."

The Ford GT40 was a rarity even in this wealthier section of town. The driver's door opened toward the sky and a man stepped out in a black suit, no tie, sporting the longer sculpted hair of a fit rock god. He left the engine idling.

"We'll put it right here in that front slot," Ramone pointed.

The man nodded. "You want me to do it for you?"

"HELL NO!"

Ramone and the man looked at Parker, who visibly shrunk. Ramone smiled.

"Sorry, he takes his job seriously."

The man smiled and tugged the lapels of his coat closer to his form. He walked around the car and toward the entrance of the restaurant.

"Hey," Parker tried to say discretely.

The man stopped.

"I gotta ask. How do you get a car like this?"

The man smiled and said in a similar, sotto voice:

"Coupons."

The man pulled open the door to Padri's and gave the hostess his name. Parker turned around to Ramone and the idling race car.

"..I fucking KNEW it!"

"Hey kid," Ramone said. Parker looked up; his olive-skinned partner held up an empty right hand.

"I do *not* care," Parker said. "Oh my God, I so want to just put this thing in gear and take it around the city a few times, just to know how it feels."

Ramone watched Parker climb into the cockpit of the monster vehicle. "It's gonna be easy to find you."

"But hard to catch!" Parker looked around at the dials and gauges. "Geez, do you know what this is Ramone?"

"A Ford GT40, I'd guess a 2005."

"Yes, that too. This," Parker said, "is an *ultimate* life hack."

Ramone leaned on the door opened toward the sky. "How do you figure?"

"Who gets to drive a car like this? Rich guys!"

"And a rich guy's valet."

"Damn right!"

"Well," Ramone said, stepping back, "I'm glad you're happy settling for fifteen feet of fame."

Ramone gently replaced the door where it belonged, closing Parker into the cockpit. He stepped quickly to the back of the car to guide Parker, mumbling *don't run me over now kid*.

Parker rolled back successfully and shut the engine down. Ramone lifted the door again.

"How was it?"

"Even in reverse it feels like a million dollars."

"A quarter million at least."

Parker climbed to his feet. He straightened up and watched as Ramone gently closed the door again. "Is that how much I just saved?"

***

After a stop by the bank to deposit his night's cut of the tips, Parker returned to his two-room flat in the hills. After a light dinner he turned on his laptop (a ten year-old Gateway he'd found on Craigslist three years ago, it still works perfectly); he went online to write in his blog, "The Diary of a Cheap Bastard:"

> *If you've ever not had money, you know there are a million ways to make five bucks last three days and still live like a baller. It's when you've got some money, and years later you still find yourself swiping coupon mailers from your neighbor's open recycling can just in case there's a cheap pizza in there somewhere, that's when you know you're hooked. I call it "Hackism."*
>
> *Of course, using only a credit card makes it even easier. Most hackers don't carry money. We prefer that money be in our minds. Banks? I see those big buildings and their cute little ATM's blinking on the corner, but taking money out of one? Not gonna happen. Account? In my mind, managed in the palm*

of my hand.

I can swagger like I've got a shit ton of money, but really if our credit cards were frozen tomorrow we'd be dead within hours. My credit is awesome, by the way, but my real value is in the ability to life-hack the shit out of everything.

Example: my first errand of the day today was to hit the pharmacy. It's 102 degrees out today so, far as I'm concerned, the grocery store's A/C comes with the price of my purchase.

So I'm standing beside the 'For patient privacy, Please wait here sign,' but when my turn comes I wave the person behind me on. Just so I can milk the A/C a little longer. I'm standing next to an end-cap display of Captain Morgan bottles that some marketing genius decided to put right next to a captive audience waiting on prescription pills.

And as I'm waiting, Don Henley's 'Boys of Summer' comes on the Muzak. I actually like that song. The best part: 99 cent download? Just saved it.

Hack.

The part that stuck with me though: the guy in line ahead of me was about 45 or so, bald, shaving to hide his ugly gene. This Gen X'er looks like the type who paid full price for Don Henley's song on cassette back in the day. Maybe even on cassette single. If he was a real hack he'd have recorded a mixed tape off the local radio station. I can't imagine a guy like him trying to live this way now. "Soon we'll all be living

like college students," I can hear him say.
Exactly! And do you remember how happy you were back then?

Parker sat to watch TV for a while after that. He remembered a drawer of unwatched DVDs beneath his entertainment center and gravitated toward the remotes. He picked up a Batman movie from the mid-90's with Jim Carey as the over-the-top Riddler. Afterward, when Parker came back and reread his blog, it didn't seem too bad. He posted it and went to bed. Tomorrow being Monday, his day off, all he had to do was show up at the rink by the airport to meet his team.

***

Every life-hacker needs a sport. Some join softball leagues. The more serious ones play some hipster sport like kickball or flag football. Something recycled from their youth made cool all over. There are adult leagues for this. Of course very few pay dues; coaches and organizers attract players and build up teams by waving fees. Those bodies on the field sometimes equate to post-game beers and tips for the waitresses. Sometimes.

Originally being from Connecticut, Parker is a hockey goalie. He's tried to resist but hockey is like a genetic predisposition. He approached this equipment-heavy sport by searching out the leg pads, skates and helmet online. The only thing he bought new was a chest protector and girdle. Anything secondhand would be caked in sweat, no matter how well-kept.

The thing that's always attracted him to the sport is the honesty of it. There's no hiding behind your amateur status when you're skating; the better guys will eat you up. And once you're too old to give or take a hit, that's it grandpa, grab a season ticket.

Now in its third year, Parker's equipment is showing its age. Last week he was in a tournament and tore a loop that holds the knee-protector strap in place. "Stupid cheap Canadian workmanship," said the forward undressing on the bench beside him.

"Might be time for new leg pads," said a defenseman. He peeled off a brand-new set of shin guards, their Velcro ripping away like fresh corn husks.

"Easy for you to say. Those things cost you."

"Thirty-seven bucks."

"These leg pads are around five hundred new, about two hundred used. Ain't got that kinda scratch. Gotta get these repaired."

"Try Red Wing shoe store," the forward said. He stripped off his jock and pulled on dry street clothes. "They've helped me milk my stuff along."

Parker took out his phone and Googled up Red Wing's address. "Thanks."

The following day he walked into the store, a torn leg pad draped over his shoulder. A man behind the counter with an Italian accent ripped a green tag in half, handed Parker half of it and wrote 'McKinney' on his half of the slip. Twelve dollars to repair a $500 set of pads. *Hack*, Parker thought to himself.

Parker pivoted to leave and almost walked into the chest of a man who'd been standing behind him. Before he could say 'excuse me' Parker lit up with recognition; it was the 45 year-old geezer from the pharmacy. Parker nodded politely but the guy seemed ready to make eye contact.

"Goalie, huh?"

"Yeah. You play?"

"Left winger." The man stuck a hand out for shaking. "Kip."

The valet shook hands. "Parker. Kip Winger," he said with a knowing smile.

The man rolled his eyes. "Jesus. No one's called me that since the 90's."

"Wasn't me. I was about six years old then."

"And yet you get the reference."

"Bad metal dies hard."

Both men nodded.

Parker felt like he needed to still say something. "You getting something repaired? Gloves, elbow pads?"

Kip the winger held up a bag, not one of those reusable grocery bags a hacker uses for pretty much everything, but a canvas bag with a draw tie, the kind a girlfriend sends you out the door with.

"Shoes," said Kip. "Need resoling."

"Hmm." So, probably a hacker after all.

"Usually I'd just replace them, but these have a certain sentimental value."

"Get them for cheap and can't part with them?"

"Wore them to my wife's funeral."

Parker's brow rose in surprise. He hadn't seen that

coming.

"Sorry man."

"It's cool. I think it's my turn," he nodded at the waiting counterman.

"Yeah, I gotta head toward the pet food place anyway."

Kip set the bag down for the guy to open. "Which store do you go to?"

"Petco. It's all about the rewards."

Kip nodded. "It's all about the information gleaning. You know those people track everything you buy and do in their place. Not to sound like an AM radio paranoid freak but sometimes, when you get something for cheap, you're giving away something else. Those reward cards... no thanks. I'll pay the extra couple bucks at the local Mom & Pop. I mean, I know he's just a dog, but some things are worth the few extra bucks."

Parker shrugged. "I couldn't disagree more, but to each his own wallet."

The counterman handed Kip a ticket and he started toward his car. "You'll see. I used to be cheap everywhere I could be, cutting corners and coupons, eating cheap, shitty food. One dirty colonoscopy and next thing you know Taco Bell is your sworn enemy."

Kip waved his claim ticket and disappeared into the parking lot. Parker watched him go. He sensed a presence at the counter behind him, having watched the whole exchange.

"Dirty colonoscopy," Parker mumbled. "Do you believe this guy? He -"

Parker swung back around, expecting a sympathetic, middle-aged Italian man. Instead he found a beautiful Italian woman, his age or younger, with naturally wavy black hair and the brownest eyes he'd ever seen.

"He's right you know."

Parker stuttered out, "I... you're... who are you?"

"Robyn, with a Y. And you're the hockey goalie."

"Yes. How did -"

"Saw the leg pad. How much did you spend on your helmet?"

"Helmet?"

"Yeah, you know, that thing protecting your head while people take slap shots at it."

"One-fifty. I could've got it cheaper but, you know, it's my head. I only get one."

"Well," said Robyn, "same goes for your colon. You get one."

"That's bullshit. I know a guy who had a whole section cut out because he had a polyp."

"And when's the last time he wore tight jeans."

"What?"

"Seriously. Does he go around in Wranglers or...?"

"No," Parker shook his head uncertainly. "He always wears..."

"Loose fitting Dockers and -"

"Sweats," Parker answered. "Always sweats."

Robyn nodded silently. "Newsflash. He isn't wearing them for comfort. It's to accommodate the diaper. Is another cheap burger really worth the likelihood of shitting yourself for life?"

***

And that's how a life-hacker changes everything in a heartbeat. Like heroin or anything else it isn't easy quitting when temptation is all around. But on a Sunday afternoon about a month later, with Robyn now squarely occupying the role of live-in girlfriend, Parker called his Uncle Curtis. When Curtis didn't answer and multiple messages went unanswered, Parker decided he was going to visit the local golf course where Curtis worked.

On his way to the front door of their apartment, Parker grabbed his driver from his golf bag and strode into the living room where Robyn was watching TV.

"I'm going to hit a bucket of balls."

Robyn jumped up, grabbed her shoes then the putter from the same golf bag. Parker shrugged and she rode beside him. At the course, Robyn was right on his hip as he walked up to the cart barn. She looked back at the driving range, then watched Parker lean into the cavernous building.

"Uncle Curtis?"

Parker's voice echoed. Every corner of the barn's cement floor was coated in the flotsam of games ended: assorted fluffy club heads detached from their owners, dozens of tees mixed with a rainbow of pencil nubs, range balls and tipped over range baskets. Carts have been hosed down, cleaned out, and put away for the night, leaving the cement floor wet as fresh rain.

The buzz of electricity filled the room as it passed through dozens of cart batteries. Everything was coated with a permanent smell of freshly cut grass.

"Curtis?"

Robyn looked at Parker. "Who's Curtis? He's your uncle?"

"Well," Parker began, then a voice said:

"Can I help you?"

A man in a Kelly green Members Only jacket and filthy gray sweats had appeared from a back room. Parker swung around.

"Uncle Curtis. It's Parker."

"Parker. I don't know any Parker."

"Your brother Tommy's son."

Curtis rolled his eyes thoughtfully, then settled on something further away.

"Oh yeah. Hey. How are you?"

Parker reintroduced himself, then Robyn, and started catching Curtis up on family happenings. All the while he could see Curtis' faraway eyes. He didn't seem to be hoping to remember anything. He just seemed to be waiting to be excused.

"Well," Parker finally said, "we're gonna go hit a few balls."

"OK."

"We'll drop your name, maybe they'll cut us a deal."

"No don't do that."

"Huh?"

"Don't... I mean, don't mention me. I try to keep a low profile, that's all."

140

"Yeah, sure," Parker nodded. "No problem. Mum's the word. Well, good seeing you Uncle Curtis."

"Yeah. Yeah, you too...

"Parker."

"Yeah. Nice meeting you Parker." Curtis turned and went back into the shack almost quickly and disappeared into the back of the cart barn.

"What. The hell. Was that," Parker said.

"I think he's living here with someone's permission, Parker."

"Hopefully." Parker started a slow confused walk back toward the clubhouse. "That was..."

"That was the guy you mentioned the day we met," Robyn guessed. "The guy in the sweats who had part of his colon removed."

Parker walked along, lost in thought. He nodded.

"Is he really your uncle?"

"Yeah. Yeah, he really is." Parker opened the door of the clubhouse for Robyn to walk thru.

"Is there, I don't know... something we should do?"

The starter appeared behind the counter. Parker pointed at the biggest basket of driving range balls they offered.

"Maybe he sees it his own way, you know? 'Hey, I get to live on a golf course and be surrounded by nature every day.'"

"No really," Robyn repeated, "is there something we should *do*?"

"Yeah," he answered her absently, "you know what

you can do?”

She looked at him.

“Bring me back here. Often.”

“Why.”

Parker grabbed his change, lifted the bucket brimming with balls, and then turned toward the beauty of the course. He gestured with his club at the starlit evening above.

“Because there's no shortcut to beauty.”

In a Flash

By

Samuel Kim

Adam peered around the corner again. He checked his camera. *Good,* he thought. Colton was approaching. Closer, closer… *FLASH!*

Colton stopped in his tracks. Blinded by the flash, he couldn't see a thing. Suddenly, he felt a sharp pain in his shin. He doubled over, moaning in pain, and fell heavily to the ground.

Adam stood over Colton. "You never thought I would get even with you, huh? Well, we're even now."

"Who are you? Huh?" Colton croaked.

Adam laughed. "This is… Adam."

Colton seethed with anger and tried to get up, but Adam had already planned for this, hence the swift and acute blow to the shin. "You!" Colton seethed, "how dare you even think of avenging me? My dad will sue you and your whole damn family in the blink of an eye! This bruise and temporary blindness is nothing compared to what I did to your pathetic life!" He groped around for Adam— without success.

Adam laughed again. Sure, the bruise and the blindness would go away, but that was not all. He smiled. As he walked away, he had a flashback to the incident Colton was referring to. He remembered it all.

***

It was his freshman year in high school. He had barely made the varsity soccer squad. It was their last game of the season. They had to win to make it to the playoffs. Adam was playing goalie. They went into double overtime. The other team got the first penalty kick.

Adam hunched down, eyes narrowing at the player from Willow Hills. The player kicked and Adam dived. It was into the wrong corner. The other team had made the goal and Adam's team had lost. After the game had ended, the captains and two mean junior jocks beat Adam up. They were angry at him for missing the goal. They ended up giving him a concussion, not to mention several bruises.

***

Colton groaned. His shin— his entire leg -- felt broken and his vision was still very foggy. He heard some footsteps and he turned to the source of the noise. Colton made out some blue and white. Adam was wearing a blue and white top, no? *He must be really stupid to come back and taunt me again. I'm going to get him this time, though.* Colton readied himself and lunged forward. He only made it two steps, for his leg was still too weak. Fortunately, the person with the blue and white top broke Colton's fall. Colton looked up. It was not Adam. It was Robert that was staring down at him.

"Colton! What were you doing there on the ground? Are you okay?"

Colton, though very embarrassed, replied, "Adam attacked me. He blinded me with his camera flash, with his stupid old camera (*who carries around cameras these days?*) and kicked me really hard in the shin."

Robert drew himself up. "He dared to get revenge on you? Wow, and he's only a sophomore… So was he still mad about the time we beat him up?"

"Yes," said Colton.

"Well, I'm going to deal with him. Where did he go?" Robert demanded.

"Uh, he went that way." Colton pointed down the hallway. Robert ran off. He sat back down and leaned against the wall. He checked his leg. It was a gross hue of purple, blue, and red.

***

Adam hurried home. He hoped no one was following him. He glanced back and saw a bobbing blue and white blob in the distance. Adam quickly brought his camera to his eyes and focused on the blob in the distance. It was… Robert! Colton's best friend! The two were the most popular senior jocks. Adam glanced at the road stretching ahead of him. It was too open. Plus, Robert was the fastest runner in the school. Adam, already having had a taste of Robert's brutality, charged into the woods by the road.

Five minutes later, an exhausted Robert threw himself onto the ground where Adam had been. He sat down, heaving with deep breaths. He saw that Adam had gone into the woods. *Should I pursue him?* Robert thought about it. Adam was clever, but he was stronger and faster. *I hope this is worth it,* thought Robert, as he dashed into the woods.

***

Adam looked back anxiously. All he saw was forest. His plan was to find Robert, blind him with his camera as well, then run home. It was going to be tricky, not to mention extremely dangerous. He was wondering if Robert was close by yet, when he nearly stumbled into a mud pit. It very wide, so there was no way he could jump over it. He looked wildly about for any fallen logs. Ah, there was one! He threw the log across the pit. He scurried over it without touching the mud, then lifted the log and threw it aside. He heard leaves rustling. Robert appeared in the distance.

The timing could not have been better. Adam stood ready. He rustled some leaves noisily to get Robert's attention. Robert saw him and made a beeline for Adam. Robert kept charging towards him, yelling, when he stumbled right into the mud pit. Robert face planted into the mud. He sputtered, and tried to get up. He howled. His favorite jeans were ruined and he was dirty all over. Worse than that, Adam had tricked him. He tried to pull himself out of the pit but it was too watery and deep. Robert bellowed as the mud started to seep into his clothes.

Adam snapped a picture of Robert. The flash blinded Robert. He thrashed about in the mud. "Delete that picture, right now!" Adam cautiously stepped towards Robert. He pulled him out of the pit. "Don't worry, my camera is broken. It can't store pictures; I just really wanted to blind you," said Adam.

Robert heaved a sigh of relief. At least Adam wasn't going to embarrass him publicly. Still, he was very angry. He sat up. He couldn't see anything, so he groped around to get up. That was a mistake because he fell into the mud pit again. He groaned. Adam pulled him back up. He lay on the ground and Adam walked away. Robert's head and heart were pounding so hard. He didn't know why, but Adam did.

***

Adam grinned. He had gotten what he wanted: revenge on Colton and Robert. He frowned as he remembered how they gave him a concussion after that soccer game, but laughed when he realized the irony of it all. He really had a camera for a reason. Not only would the flash temporarily blind the victim, it would also give the unfortunate subject a permanent migraine. That was it, though. Adam was merciful.

***

Colton typed rapidly on his phone. He texted Robert, "Hey, this is really weird. After Adam blinded me, I have had an incessant headache. It's driving me nuts. I also feel really dizzy and weak. What about you?"

Robert's response frightened him.

"Yeah, me too. He blinded me in the forest after I fell into the mud pit. Made me ruin my brand new jeans. My headache isn't going away and I keep having the feeling that I am being watched. I just feel really restless."

Colton was about to text Robert back, when another message from him came.

"Yeah, and I Googled some of the symptoms, and guess what? We might have radiation poisoning."

Radiation poisoning?!?!?

Not a Care in the World

By

Matthew Aufiero

Alex watched a cultist surreptitiously check the underside of a rock from a monitor at the police precinct headquarters. Alex gave another *loooong* sigh as he watched the cultist. He already knew there was an illegal pistol and ammo taped to the underside of the rock which the cultist would illegally use to practice shooting, and he didn't care. Alex had been watching the cultist, and the cult that he was a member of, for months in the hopes of catching them in the act of some bigger crime. They had already been responsible for the disappearance of several families and he had to make sure that they didn't do anything else.

The train of thought ended abruptly as his phone rang.

"Alex what do you have?" his boss said.

"Not much yet, well not enough to really get them," Alex replied timorously.

"Well get it. Or maybe you'll be better at working traffic," his boss said with a deadpan voice before hanging up the phone. Alex leaned back and sighed. The call had come in right on schedule, just like every other day and, just like every other day, it had a way of heaping stress onto Alex. He turned his attention back to the monitors. The cult mansion was a sore thumb in the middle of an immaculate

149

neighborhood with its messy lawns, peeling paint, and rotting wood juxtaposed with its perfectly kept neighbors.

"Josh, you haven't checked in for a while. Give me something," Alex said with an air of boredom, while switching his screen to a different camera which allowed him to view the cultist mansion and the stakeout car in which Josh was watching. Nothing was going to happen and he knew it, but it was all for the record.

"Well, we ran outta coffee, so Denise went to get some more," Josh said with a similar attitude.

"From where?" Alex responded not really caring enough to find out.

"There's a nice coffee shop like five minutes away from here."

"Okay," Alex concluded. Another ten minutes passed by. Then another. After another ten minutes Alex finally said, "Well, did she ever come back?"

"Uh no, I'm going to, oh shi-"

"What? What happened?" Alex said, nervously scanning the cameras. And then he saw Denise in the backyard of the cult mansion talking to one of the senior members.

"DENISE, WHAT THE HELL ARE YOU DOING?" Alex screamed into the microphone.

"OW, sir I don't think she can hear us. She took her earpiece off," Josh said.

"Why would she do that? She's going to blow the entire operation!"

"I don't know why!"

"Dammit. Wait there until she comes back. I'm

sending in some backup."

Alex rushed into the small room that was the headquarters of the operation. He saw Tom asleep and Lucy watching TV.

"Denise went in," Alex said.

Lucy turned and looked at him with unconcealed surprise.

"You said we weren't going undercover," she said, accusation in her voice.

"Yeah, well Denise thought otherwise, and you need to get there in case we need to get her out."

Lucy sighed then went to get ready. Alex slapped Tom and told him to talk to Lucy. He ran back to the monitor.

"Josh, has she come back yet?"

"No, I think she went inside the actual mansion," Josh said with the same air of panic. "Oh my god--I killed her! When she went for that coffee, it's like I put a bullet straight through her head."

"Calm down, dammit. This isn't your fault. She went in, she took the risk, and she's getting suspended. Lucy are you on your way?"

"Yes, do you have to yell?"

"YES!"

"Alright, but I sent Tom to get some coffee-"

"WHAT?"

"OW, Jesus, I just sent Tom to get some coffee--what's the big deal? I doubt anything's going to happen anyways."

Alex brought up the front door monitor and sure

enough, Tom was walking straight through the door of the mansion.

"SON OF A BITCH!" Alex shouted through the comms. "Everyone stay put, no more coffee, just stay in the car and don't do anything."

"Is this a bad time to say that Lucy went to get coffee?" Josh said.

"It's like I'm running a circus full of monkeys. Even monkeys could probably stake out a house better then you guys. Follow Lucy and see what the hell is up with this damn coffee."

"Okay," Josh said and then silence for a minute.

"Say something Josh. JOSH!"

"Nothing's happening, she's just getting the--wait a minute--she must be really into this cashier. She's been talking with him for five minutes straight. Oh, he's handing her something. It looks like he's handing her a card. She's...smiling? I don't understand, she never has this much fun just getting coffee."

"Alright, I'm going over there now. Wait before you do anything and for chrissake, NO COFFEE."

Before Josh replied, Alex was headed out the door, grabbing enough guns for the whole team and a lot of ammo, just in case. *I am not going to play around with these bastards*, was the only thought looping through his mind. He sped through traffic and parked haphazardly on the curb of the cult mansion and raced through the unkempt front lawn. He stopped at the door and took one second to catch his breath and to smooth out his suit. The door had looked impressive, large for five to enter side-by-side, but now its blue paint peeled, its wood sagged and rotted, and its bronze knockers were dulled. Alex knocked on the door, and it swung open, completely unlocked and not even properly shut.

Without hearing any response or reply he crept forward on his toes ready to draw his gun at any moment and fire.

He found a door and peeked through. It looked like a living room, but he couldn't quite get a good look.

The door opened and Alex jerked back hiding behind the wall.

"This is detective Alex from the SAPD. We have your building surrounded. Let go of the hostages and come out with your hands interlaced behind your head," Alex said with has much authority as he could muster.

"No you don't, we have no hostages, please come in," said an odd voice with an eastern accent, but a lethargic drawl more commonplace in the Deep South.

Well damn. It was worth a shot. "Okay your building isn't surrounded *yet*, but that can change quickly so let the hostages go and we'll see what we can do about not pressing kidnapping charges."

"We don't have any hostages. I presume you're talking about the other policemen that came in earlier. They're fine--"

"Bullshit, you bring them out here right now and there better not be a mark on them," Alex said, cocking his pistol. He heard the cultist take some steps, and Alex held his breath.

"They don't want to come right now. They have not

objected to seeing you, however, so you are welcome to come in and see them," the same bored voice drawled back.

"Sounds like quite the trap. How about I come back with a SWAT team and see if they want to come in then?"

"You're welcome to come in whenever you want."

Damn it. I don't want to charge into a house of crazy people, but I can't leave my idiot teammates in there. He breathed for a minute and then peeked through again. He found a relatively safe hiding spot, then sprinted there. It was behind a massive black leather couch inside of a living room, as he had suspected, large and cozy, filled with many more couches and seats. Alex checked his sightlines, a little rusty since he hadn't been in a firefight for years. His partners were... lying on the couch, eating chocolate cake.

"WHAT THE HELL ARE YOU DOING?" Alex shouted.

"Nothing," Denise said, lying supine with at least two empty plates.

"WHY ARE YOU JUST LYING THERE EATING GODDAMN CAKE?" Alex shouted.

"Allow me to introduce myself over a short walk," a familiar voice said. "I am Peter Stewart. Please put away your weapon. Some of the other members of the group might be afraid."

"Just go talk to him," Denise said with an air of impatience.

"I'm confused," Alex said.

"I promise you that no one will be hurt," Peter said.

Alex looked at Denise for a while, then looked at Peter, watching each for signs of artifice. He nodded and dropped his gun to his side, being as careful to show it was still out and ready. Peter opened a door and led Alex out to a garden towards a gazebo that Alex had spied many times through the cameras.

"Let me start off first. We have a short, but storied history. My uncle started this place in the sixties, but due to the Red Scare he was afraid that people would associate us with the Communists," Peter said like a tour guide describing a museum exhibit.

"Started what? What is the point of your little cult?"

"I would hesitate to call us a cult. We don't really have any religious affiliation."

"Then what is the point?" Alex said with increasing impatience.

"Please let me finish. You see my uncle was a very, very rich man--made his fortune off of apples--and yet life just seemed empty. He had it all -- a wife, children, money. But he came to an interesting conclusion. What was it he said? Ah yes, *he didn't give a shit*." Here Peter laughed. "It made the rest of the family quite angry, but he paid no mind. He had this house built, sold all his stocks, and moved here to find what it was he really cared about. His children now run similar organizations in a few other cities and his wife is here in this building."

"I don't understand. Why the cult then?"

"We're not a cult, more of a lifestyle. My uncle called the lifestyle 'Not caring-ism.' He might've had business savvy, but he was never one for words."

"But the disappearances?"

"Oh those were just the more advanced members of the cult. They are more or less fine, camped out in the various rooms of the mansions. They took the tenets of our philosophy to heart and now I don't think they ever leave the rooms. I, myself, was never quite able to leave all of my cares behind. I suppose that makes me a horrible teacher of not caring, eh?"

Alex did not respond, stupefied. He watched the unkempt trees of the backyard, the overgrown grass, the wild butterflies.

"How do you even keep this running? I mean somebody has to be paying for something right?"

"Yes, of course. Those people my uncle sold his stocks to were more than happy to join up. Only for a few, business was a passion, and they kept at it. And even then, many of our members work as they want to, only doing the jobs they want. When something is too unclean for human conditions, somebody cleans it. When someone is hungry, they make food and maybe enough food for others. It is remarkable how good people become when they are free of worry or anxiety."

"I just don't understand. This can't be right."

"I couldn't tell you about that. I'm not much of a philosopher, but I can tell you that it's great to not care."

Again, a long pause and Alex turned to watch the sky, while Peter clasped a flower in his palms.

"But then how did the others get indoctrinated?" Alex said.

"Well, we knew about this for a while--"

"What? How?"

"Your janitor is a card-carrying member. So is the barista of the coffee shop which is frequented by an inordinate amount of policemen on stake-out. He is actually one of our more persuasive members. Pity he doesn't wish to be an orator, he might just be one of the best. Ah well, I can't fault him for perusing his life's passion, even if it is only to make coffee."

"I still don't understand," Alex said quietly, almost whispering.

"I don't either. But for right now, if you want, just try thinking about what you really want in life, even if it is just a childish fancy. After all, Denise only wants to eat chocolate cake, and she almost never gets up, except to make some."

"But I have responsibilities."

"Not nearly as many as you think. Listen, I don't care if you join our 'cult.' Perhaps it isn't perfect and it does have flaws--poor Denise will end up obese--but it works now and the beauty is that we are all very accepting of change. I'll come back in a little while."

Peter left, leaving Alex alone with his questions. Alex sat trying to fight each one in turn, unmoving and silent. He knew that the "cult" was at least responsible for assisted suicide if nothing else. He knew that it couldn't possibly work out. That the cult was an idyllic fantasy, that letting go of responsibility or worry was reckless, even dangerous. Hell, all he ever wanted to do was be a policeman, and that hadn't changed before or after Peter's speech.

As he saw Peter walk out of the mansion and on to the stone-stepping path which led to the gazebo, his phone rang.

"What's going on? I've been hearing a lot of crazy

stuff from others at the station? ANSWER ME!"

As Alex listened to the growing anxiety in his boss's voice, he suddenly realized...*he just didn't care.*

A Nature Story
By
Anne Wilson

Approach the lake; please see me.

Under confetti sprays of giant hogweed, through comfrey and nettles, purple loosestrife and Indian balsam you may see me. I am always here.

I am waiting, but tread with care; wet grasses and bright marsh marigolds, reeds and rushes, all are rooted in unsafe shallows.

My hair changes style, this way and that, as Mother Nature takes back the dark tresses she gave me. I have a halo of tiny water-crowfoot, cast over the water's surface like a reflection of the Milky Way across the night sky. It sweeps away from my floating hair like a ghostly bridal veil.

Relieved of the onerous responsibility for my own appearance, I am a work in progress contrived by Mother Nature. The dead evolve to a prescribed formula; wearing much the same patterns and changing as each other; mauves to purple, bruised puce, chartreuse and sage green, grey to black.

Snatches of memory still flicker like fireflies in the dark, only to extinguish as I try to hold on to them. They flit away into the umbra that is all my tomorrows. I used to imagine faces, always distorted, then they were gone.

Occasionally small whimsical ghosts, dimly recalled images of my previous life, pay me a visit. They scud across the water, dancing and skipping; plastic carriers, packets and cartons. Some catch in the reeds and become waterlogged but some remain free to continue their travels, bowling along, lifting in the air. Some are biodegradable like me. Last winter there was a letter; I would have liked to read the words but was unable to do so. The pages floated for a while then sank; that day I felt very alone.

Did I have a family? I have certainly given birth to the offspring of others. I have sheltered their eggs and nourished their fat writhing larvae. I have provided a home for creatures I did not know existed, where the spectre at the feast *is* the feast.

Please see me.

I have hosted banquets for a great many water snails. They consume decomposing matter so I suppose the unread letter became a tasty snack; perhaps an hors d'oeuvre before the greater repast. My parasites are too legion to list. They are a diabolical army sent to devour defenceless flesh.

My eyeballs were the first to go, yet I can see the amoeba inhabiting a single water droplet, the beauty of morning dewdrops decorating a spider's web. I can wonder at the wisdom of the tiny creature that calculated during construction for this additional weight.

I can watch as the floating bladderwort uses its roots to catch and kill the tiny life-forms that are its underwater prey.

Primitive water fleas rush hither and thither oblivious to all about them. Water-boatmen, skating on the water's skin, come close enough for me to see their tiny nightmarish faces around my cumbersome torpid mass as I dissolve into their watery world; in winter gelid; in summer fetid.

I was discovered once by a family of rodents. They ate their fill, until something spooked them and they did not return.

Water spiders come from their underwater nests of bubbles to walk on water, some with one hundred eggs in their silken egg bags. They scuttle over me, their touch as light and delicate as the wings of the flies they will consume for breakfast; flies that have ingested my flesh and waste. One such creature, the poor mayfly, lives its whole life in just twenty-four hours.

By day, curlews and larks rise from the water meadows. Birds cheer my spirit with their calls; blue jays, thrushes and nightingales. Woodpeckers drill their staccato beat exploring tree bark for grubs. As the brilliant plumage of the kingfisher flashes from the alders by the lake side, its whistling call vibrates the air.

When darkness falls, creatures of the night emerge and circle the lake: foxes, badgers, bats and owls. *They* do not sense *me* but their stealthy tread and silently beating wings are a nocturne audible to those of my kind; but they have nothing to fear from me.

All night long, I hear as the wind rustles and scratches through the rushes like a quill pen exhorted to endlessly record the passage of time. It whistles, sighs and moans like lost souls seeking the light.

In summer, the flower meadows hum with insect life and the jewel colours of butterfly wings. Fritillaries seek the damp grasslands; the Orange Tip seeks cuckoo flowers and garlic mustard; the Duke of Burgundy hunts out cowslips on which to lay its eggs and the Large Heath flutters in the dancing tufts of cotton-sedge at the water's edge. Many varieties seek stinging nettles as hosts for their larvae but one hunts out my corpse for sustenance. The large, majestic Purple Emperor lives and spawns among the willows and aspens that border the lake but this beautiful creature is not seeking nectar; it feeds only on putrescence, on excrement and gore.

In winter, when the moon has a gauzy halo and temperatures drop to freezing, a grey winter world emerges around me. Tree branches reach out stripped of their leaves, black in the moonlight. Rain and ice weigh down the frozen grasses and swell the water level of the lake. I can revel in the violence of sudden storms orchestrated in the heavens, when howling winds stream through the air, lightning flashes in the hills and down-pours pelt my cadaver with frenzied rage.

I can sense the pulsing hearts of cold clusters of sheep sheltering on the fells; their wool crusted with snow, their breath vaporising around them in a pink dawn light.

Last summer's broken bracken is clusters of pale brown stalks topped by clumps of snow and ice crystals, bent into organic ice sculptures. As winter lingers, everything waits for the temperature to rise; for the snow and ice to retreat. The air is bright and dry. Hidden, just beneath the topsoil, are nature's first tiny green shoots.

I hear the secretive cuckoo herald spring with its distinctive call. It has survived the killing of the natural offspring of the parents who succoured it. Nature can be an unkind and cruel mother.

I grow closer to natural things as I become absorbed into them; links in a never-ending chain of sparking life.

After stasis came rigour mortis; then chaos. I am in chaos, some parts moribund but still nutritious to some species; some parts already a fusion with other organisms. My transformation continues but you have passed me by.

I can no longer remember how I came here; what sequence of events left me alone and trapped, embraced by twisted roots. It may have been by my own deed or misadventure. It may have been by the hand of another. I know I harbour ill-will to no one and soon I will end my vigil, no longer anchored by old and pointless emotions, memories and attachments to the existential world. The mantle of agitation over worldly issues left unresolved has melted away.

Soon my spirit will be free to explore infinity, to wander into the void where the wild things are, heading for the edges of the universe. I will transcend matter, into the cosmos, weightless and free.

You have failed to see me, but perhaps there are those remaining on Earth who will remember me in their dreams.

Spencer

By

Catherine A. MacKenzie

A woman I once knew wasn't at all like a woman. She went by the name of Spencer (her last name was Krametszy), and she was a monster of a person, both in appearance and personality.

I don't think Spencer had ever frequented a hair salon. Instead, I think she hacked at her hair with her own scissors. She desperately needed one of those hot oil treatments. Her shoulder length, fake blonde hair was as flyaway as a kite in a hurricane. Most definitely she could have used a manicure and pedicure, but I never faulted her for that. Not every woman wore nail polish.

When Spencer spoke, bubbles formed at the corners of her mouth and spittle flew across the room. One had to be lucky to avert the spray. She could have had a speech defect, I suppose, but I had the impression she simply became excited when someone paid attention to her and then she couldn't get her words out fast enough, afraid the person would walk away. Sometimes she even grabbed an individual's arm as if to ensure that person didn't bolt.

I found her boring, and I can't stand boring people. When she spoke, spittle and spray notwithstanding, I yawned. She was *that* boring. My husband, Hal, found her interesting, but I could relax since I didn't have to compete with Spencer. I didn't have to worry about my husband carrying on with her as he did with other females—he'd never be interested in someone like her. But that's another story; a mundane, ordinary tale, not nearly as interesting as that of Spencer.

Unlike me, Spencer rarely wore jeans or slacks. She preferred short, tight skirts or form-fitting dresses over her large, obnoxious frame held up by thick tree-stump legs. Standing beside her, I felt svelte, young, and beautiful, even though I didn't consider myself particularly attractive nor did I have the world's best figure. At 147 pounds and five foot five, I was fat and frumpy. I've always thought it ironically funny how the fattest women wear the tightest and skimpiest clothing. Looking back, time spent with Spencer was the only time my ego was boosted.

One morning, just when I had stepped from the shower, the phone rang.

"Let's go downtown. Have lunch," Spencer said.

Really? I didn't know how to reply. She and I had never gone out previously without our husbands, and I had been rude to her the last time we had been together when I said something like, "Maybe you should look in the mirror before you leave the house." As usual, I had had too much to drink; the booze spoke, not me. Hal had chastised me like crazy after we returned home.

Perhaps Spencer was hard up. We weren't close, and I had never met her friends—if she had any. She was married to Gary Chichester, a co-worker of Hal's, which is how we had met. Hal, although he liked her, had mentioned once that she must be wonderful in bed for Gary to be married to her. "Really?" I had said. "That's all it takes? Good sex?"

Spencer waited for my reply. "Okay," I said. I didn't have anything to do that day, and the kids wouldn't be home from school until 3 o'clock.

"I'll meet you at Sundial Mall then. Ten o'clock. That okay?"

I glanced at the clock. Just a bit before nine. "Okay, sounds good."

Spencer was waiting for me at Creamfield's Donuts, which was by the main entrance. *Oh yeah, likely delving into creamy goodness for the last thirty minutes,* I thought.

"Hey," she said. "Glad you could meet me."

I stayed as far away from her as I could without appearing obnoxious. I'd already had a shower; I didn't need another.

"I want to look for some new clothes. I need a new look."

Ya, you think? "Sure," I said. "I'd be glad to help."

"I thought perhaps Elaine's."

Elaine's was one of the preeminent clothing stores in the mall, and the only one to carry plus sizes.

"Okay."

We sauntered through the mall. I glanced in a couple of stores, noticing our reflection in the glass and wondering if I looked as embarrassed as I felt. Somehow, I didn't feel that self-conscious when she and I were out with our husbands. I suppose the alcohol helped at those times, for the four of us met for dinner and drinks and not much else.

"Here we are," Spencer puffed from the exertion of the short walk.

"Yippee," I mumbled.

"What?" she said.

I didn't reply, and she walked over to the large woman section. She fingered the silky fabric of a dress and then touched a frilly pink blouse on an adjacent rack. "What do you think of this?"

"Um...." I wasn't sure what to say. I didn't think pink was her colour, but she wore a lot of it. "What about this blue one?" The blouse had the same frills.

"No, I think pink suits me better, don't you think?"

Whatever you think.

She pulled out a pink and white low-cut dress and held it in front of her. "Do you think this one would look good?" Even though a plus size, I thought the bodice would be too revealing for her—or for any woman, for that matter. I wanted to ask why she enjoyed flaunting herself, especially unattractive body parts, but I kept my mouth firmly clenched. I didn't have liquor to fall back on.

"Try it on," I said.

"I just might. Let me find a couple more to make it worthwhile."

She grabbed another three outfits and thundered to the dressing room. Not knowing what else to do, I followed.

The saleswoman eyed Spencer before taking the clothes from her and leading us into the spacious fitting area. She opened the door to a cubicle and Spencer disappeared. I sat on the plush couch and waited. Spencer and I were the only ones there. While I waited, I stared at a gaudy painting.

I glanced back and saw her bare feet below the door. What was taking so long? Obviously she wasn't going to model the outfits or she'd have been out by now. She must be determining by herself if they fit or not, which suited me. I had no desire to tell her how she looked, good or bad.

"You okay in there?" I finally asked, regretting my words as soon as I had said them.

"A bit of trouble getting this one zipped up."

I remained silent. I didn't want to help.

The fitting room door opened. Spencer wore a flowing red dress and clutched the fabric up over her boobs as if the mounds would burst forth if she let go.

"Can you zip me up?"

"Okay," I said. When she turned around, I stepped toward her.

Everything happened in slow motion. You know how that is—when something you don't want to see presents itself and the sight is so unfathomable you can't tear your eyes away though all you want to do is close your eyes and run for your life. That's how it was with me that day. A visual I didn't want to see—and never want to see again— revealed itself to me. I suppose I should have clued in previously.

To this day, I don't quite know how the unfortunate incident happened. Somehow, Spencer tripped and, in order to remain upright, dropped the dress she had held across her breasts. And when she did, she exposed herself above her waist—an image I'll never forget, an image forever engraved in my mind like a gory scene from a horror movie.

Were those swaying pendulums really breasts? They hung where breasts exist, but they didn't resemble breasts. Deep pink scars were prominent on too-white flesh. Then I felt like a shit when I suddenly realized she could have kicked cancer before enduring breast reconstructive surgery. Or perhaps she had had a breast augmentation or a reduction. Yes that was it; not cancer after all. Then no, I thought—not a reduction because the breasts were still too big.

As if that first sight wasn't enough for innocent eyes, the second was even more frightful.

"Eek!" At some point during the scene, Spencer screeched as if she had seen a rat before dawning registered on her face. The dress then fell from her waist to the floor. (How it had slipped off her chunky frame will always remain a mystery.) She leaned over in her ugly monstrosity to cover her exposed genitalia, but she wasn't quite quick enough. (Another unsolved mystery will be why she wasn't wearing underwear.)

Eyes bulging, her face turned scarlet and then white. Her mouth formed into a grimace. Embarrassment morphed into horror as if she had watched the same terrifying movie that I had. Yet it was me who saw the scene, not her. I experienced that sight for the first time, one she had been privy to. It was I—me—who should have sported her terrified look, which I'm sure I did. My eyes had to have been as big as dollar coins and my mouth a perfect "O."

Before me was a man, not a woman. I suppose she could have been a wanna-be-woman in the throes of change. But how could Hal and I not have known? How could we have dined with that couple and not known their secret?

Spencer and Gary moved away shortly after the incident, but not as fast as I had bolted from the store. Later, Hal told me Gary had obtained a transfer to California. She—he?—would be better able to finish her treatments there—and obtain the obviously essential surgery to correct a badly botched operation.

Yes, I knew a woman once, only she wasn't a real woman. Not really.

Broadcast Emotion

By

Glen Damien Campbell

Night or day, Vic's curtains were always drawn. Like a vampire in its diurnal lair Vic kept his windows painstakingly covered, never allowing even the slightest slither of light from the world beyond to sneak through. The idea of people from the outside being able to peep in on him through even the tiniest of portals was terrifying to Vic. Though really this shouldn't have been a concern; his tiny apartment was located on the eighteenth floor of his graffiti riddled, dog-shit smeared high rise council tower. The only things that passed by his windows, besides the drug paraphernalia and cigarette butts discarded by the squatters in the apartment above his, were birds and they cared more about crapping on his windows than what was going on behind them. But nevertheless, Vic kept his curtains drawn for, as irrational as it may sound, he knew that somewhere "out there" in the ether was an almighty power, an all seeing eye, a primordial, unknowable nosey bastard, and Vic did not want whatever that thing was to see what a miserable state his life was in. He didn't want *it* to know that *it* was winning.

The chintzy wallpaper, inherited from the incontinent septuagenarian who had lived (and died) in the apartment before Vic, peeled from the damp walls in the living room. The room was cold and dark, the centre light bulb had blown weeks ago, and so the mesmeric pale glow of Vic's large outdated television set provided the room's only illumination. A product two decades past its prime, from a time when manufacturers hadn't yet begun placing self-destruct time bombs in their products, Vic's television was practically an antique. Nowadays everyone but him seemed to have one of them high-definition, smarter-than-you, plasma super-duper flat screen TVs. Vic knew he needed to get one of them soon. The only problem was he couldn't afford one. So until he could he was forced to remain a technological outcast. That was another reason why he kept the curtains closed. *The techno-Nazis were out there!*

It was eight minutes past nine. The nine o'clock news was on the telly. A smarmy looking anchorman with a coiffure that looked like it belonged in MOMA was reading out the day's headlines with the usual broadcaster's dispassion. Opposite the TV, slouched upon the couch and bathing in the television's flickering radiance, were Vic and his two friends, Sam and Preston.

With countenances that suggested both irritation and apathy, the three men stared ahead into the cyclopean brilliance of the TV screen wishing that they were watching something else. *"Why Are You So Fat?"* was on the other station and all three men would rather have been watching that. It was an elimination show today. One of the dieting fatties was going to be voted off and shown the door. Whether or not they would then be able to fit through that door was the fun of watching.

The news, however, was unusual viewing for the

trio. If they wanted to hear about drugs, guns, murder, rape, and terrorism they could have put their ears up against the walls and listened to the neighbours. The only reason they were watching the news now was because the batteries in the television remote control were dead and no one was volunteering to get up and change the channel manually. And so, because of their inveterate laziness, they were left compelled to listen to the cleft-chinned reporter mechanically inform them of the goings-on of the world via the promptings of his auto-cue.

"Scientists at the Psychology University in London have today published findings of a study into the mental health of the nation," read the anchorman. "Conducted over the course of six years, the findings suggest that one in three males, between the ages of eighteen and fifty, will at some point in their life suffer a severe psychotic episode."

Vic budged uncomfortably in his seat. Shifting his eyes askance, he peeked to his left at Sam and then peeked to his right at Preston. Surprisingly, the faces of his two friends were as blank as ever. Unlike him they did not seem to realise the implications of what had just been reported to them. Just to be sure, as clandestinely as he could, Vic did a recount with his finger. Yes, there were definitely three of them. That was the first box ticked. In addition to that, they were all between eighteen and fifty years in age. That ticked off the second box. They ticked all the boxes! So what did that mean? It meant that one them was a ticking time bomb, a sleeper psychopath just waiting to be triggered. Only which one of them was it, wondered Vic as he began to scratch his forearm nervously.

First, he considered Sam, the forty-year old virgin who still lived with his mother even though she had been dead now for four years. He was a definite Norman Bates candidate. But, just as likely, was Preston, the socialist postal worker from Liverpool who shared a shabby one room studio apartment with two roommates who both worked in the sex industry. And by "worked in the sex industry," what is actually meant is that they were both blow up dolls.

Clearly, both Stan and Preston were first-rate potential psychopaths. But what really bothered Vic was that, knowing his luck, when the twig was finally snapped in the psycho's head he'd probably be the victim.

"Another beer anyone?" asked Vic, hiding the consternation he was feeling behind a cheery tenor.

"Yeah I'll have another," said Sam.

Of course *he* would have another, greedy bastard, thought Vic. Sam was always happy to take but never happy to bring any beers himself.

"Me too," said Preston, who was just as greedy a bastard as Sam. "And change the channel while you're up, this is depressing. Put it on the show about the fat fuckers."

Up off the couch, Vic changed the channel as requested and then headed off towards the kitchenette to get the beers. Judging by his rate of alcohol consumption Preston, it seemed, was determined to get wasted. He'd probably go home tonight drunk and rowdy, get into an argument with one of his blow up dolls and end up puncturing it in the face again.

The three beers Vic pulled out of the fridge were

warm even though they had been cooling in there for over two hours. Like everything in Vic's life, the fridge had broken down. Setting the beers down upon the kitchen counter, Vic looked up at the moldy, speckled ceiling and sighed.

With it all but certain that one of his guests was a latent psychopath, Vic was nervous about resuming his seat upon the couch. He could ask them to leave perhaps, but Vic soon dismissed that idea; doing something like that could very well be what triggers the psychotic breakdown. Where there's psychosis there's paranoia. If Vic was to start acting strangely now the psycho might think he was being plotted against and freak out. So what could he do? Just play along and act like everything's fine until the inevitable mental meltdown? No, that would not do; no one should live their life in fear. There was only one thing for it. Vic opened the cutlery drawer and began to rummage for a suitably large knife. To be on the safe side, decided Vic, he would have to kill them both.

Luckily, due to his fondness for butcher off-cuts, Vic's cutlery drawer held two carbon steel meat cleavers. For what he had in mind they would do nicely. With a cleaver in each hand, Vic slunk up behind the living room couch, elevated the blades above the heads of its two occupants, Sam and Preston, and then brought them down. Like ripe cantaloupes, he split their heads in twain simultaneously. Preston died instantly. Sam, however, by virtue of being on the receiving end of Vic's weaker left hand strike, went into spasms. It was the most animated Vic had ever seen him. But another whack of the cleaver immediately put an end to it. Then, sitting back down upon the couch between the two bleeding corpses, Vic leaned back, cracked open a warm beer with his blood splattered hands and watched the telly. *"Why Are You So Fat?"* was on.

Fork Story

By

Mary Steer

The tines of the fork were hurting her ass. She smiled sweetly across the table at Allan who narrowed his eyes in response.

"Everything okay?" he asked.

"Oh, yes," she said.

"Because you're looking at me funny."

"Sorry—didn't mean to." She looked down again at her meal. Shit. He'd used her fork, not his. Well, she'd show him. She selected a spear of asparagus, picking it up daintily between finger and thumb.

"What are you doing?"

She looked up. He was smirking. She lifted one shoulder and let it drop. "You're supposed to eat asparagus with your fingers. Didn't you know?"

That wiped the smirk off his face. But she only had three spears of asparagus—stupid minimalist nouvelle cuisine—and then she'd have to find a way to cope with the curried chicken and rice.

Could she eat them with her fingers too, and tell him that's how they do it in India?

No. She could, but she didn't want to. She had to make a move. She shifted slightly and felt the tines dig a little deeper—yes, she really had to make a move. Mind you, it could've been worse. She could've sat just slightly farther back on the chair and really regretted it.

Allan was staring at her.

"Aren't you hungry?" she asked him.

"Oh," he said. "Oh, yeah." And he picked up his own fork and began to eat. Bastard.

"You don't have any horseradish," she pointed out.

He looked at his plate for a moment, then shrugged. "I don't need horseradish."

"You never eat beef without horseradish. Shall I go get a server?"

"No, no, one will come by in a minute and we can ask then."

So that didn't work. She should've been more forceful—she should've remembered not to ask but to tell: I'll go get a server. Of course he would decline an offer. She tried to think of something else. She couldn't go to the washroom again. It was stupid to go the first time but she'd really needed to.

Wait a minute. There was nothing to say, she couldn't really need to go more than once—

"Where are you going now?" There was that nasty little smirk again, the corners of his mouth just lifted but no teeth showing, the first two wrinkles on either side of his eyes deepening into creases.

"The ladies'."

"You just went."

Standing now, she didn't dare rub her ass—she could only hope the tines hadn't pulled any threads in her skirt or left noticeable dents in the fabric. "It's not very delicate of you to comment, you know," she told him. "I can go into detail if you like, but let's just say my stomach is a bit upset."

His expression turned gloating and triumphant, his eyes cried Liar! She walked away from the table knowing he was watching her go, knowing he was examining her rear for signs of damage. Score: 1-0. They really didn't get out often enough—she was out of practice. How was it he never had to go to the bathroom, never left the table to track down a server?

Her only option was defensive action, and this was tough when you weren't sure what the next offensive might be. Would there be more silverware hidden on her seat in the darkened restaurant when she went back? Or would it be something on the table—like a floatie in her wine? A hair, an eyelash perhaps, on the butter on her side dish?

She gazed at her reflection as she rubbed the prong-marks on her bum. Was there any way to steal the offensive from him? A thought occurred. She turned and left the safety of the bathroom once again.

When she returned to the table, she smoothed her chair carefully before sitting down.

"What're you doing?" he asked as she ran her hands over the padded surface.

"You're full of questions this evening," she said mildly. "I thought I saw some crumbs on my seat." She drew her hands over her buttocks, tucking in her skirt as she slid her knees under the table, and as she did so she nudged the tabletop, tipping over his glass of water so it spilled all over his lap. He cursed softly.

"I'm so sorry."

"That's all right. It was an accident." He was

grinning. "I'll just get a waiter to bring an extra napkin." He made no move to rise.

"Oh no, it was my bad. I'll go get one for you." She stood up and hurried off. Once she'd found a server and secured a napkin from him, she made a pit stop in the bathroom on the way back to the table.

"Here," she said, "you can blot it with this—" and she dropped the napkin, soapy side down, into his lap. His eyes widened for a moment—but just for a moment.

"Thank you," he said, his features smooth and imperturbable once more. He was looking up at her, waiting for her rejoin him at the table.

She remained on her feet, looking down at him, trying to suss out the situation in her peripheral vision. She should never have got up that third time. She'd left herself open—and had the soapy napkin really been worth it?

"Are you sure you won't need another napkin? I can go get more—I should've brought more than one." She was still surreptitiously scanning the table.

"Please sit," he said. "Your dinner's getting cold. I'll be fine."

Sure enough, she had no cutlery at all—God knew where he'd put it—and there was a grain of curried rice in her water.

"I'm not sure we locked the car," she said. "I'll just go check."

"Oh, I'm sure it's locked."

"No, I don't think so."

"But there's nothing of value in it. Don't worry about it. Please, come and eat with me." He smiled beguilingly.

"I'd better check on the babysitter first," she said. "Since I'm on my feet. I'll take it outside so I don't disturb anyone."

He looked enraged for a moment, but quickly smoothed the anger from his face and managed to smile again, if a little tightly. "Of course—good idea." Rules of the game. He could tell her he was sure the car was locked, or that she shouldn't worry about it if it wasn't, but he knew he wasn't allowed to point out that they didn't have any kids.

Outside, she breathed in a couple of lungfuls of cold, fresh air. She had to think of something new. She had to get her cutlery back. She had to get him on his feet so she had the upper hand.

Got it.

Back inside the restaurant, she waved a server over.

"How can I help?"

She sighed. "My husband and I are sitting over there," she said, indicating around the corner by the reception desk. "I'm really not comfortable sitting there." This was not a lie. "My husband hates to make a fuss, but I notice you're not very busy this evening, and I wondered if it would be all right if we switched to this table," she pointed, "over here?"

The briefest look of doubt and confusion flitted across the server's face, instantly replaced by a calm and placid confidence.

"Certainly, we can do that for you," he replied.

"Oh, goody," she said. "I'll wait here."

Seven minutes went by before Allan arrived at the

table, carrying his wine, trying to clear a thunderous look from his face, and followed by two servers carrying their food, her wine, and one glass of water. He must have put up quite the struggle.

The server she had asked to move their table was apologetic. "I'm sorry, I don't know where your cutlery went, but I'll bring you some more. And a fresh glass of water." He wouldn't admit to the floatie, but that was normal. Servers often played the game too.

Allan looked down on her. "More comfortable here?"

"Oh yes. Yes indeed. Please sit down. I'm fine now."

It was a measure of how thoroughly she'd rattled him that he sat down without checking his chair. His grimace was fleeting. She gave him a radiant smile.

Tuneism
By
David Perlmutter

One poster taped to the left side of a wall revealed the message. The other, on the right, the messenger.

They covered the entire wall for, apparently, a good reason.

The messenger was a girl somewhere between the ages of eight and twelve; I can't be sure. She was wearing what looks like a pair of pajamas, yellow and purple in color, and a blue bicycle helmet over her head. But what is rather extraordinary is that she was lifting a giant rock with her right hand- and *only* her right hand. The left was simply at her side, not needed.

She seemed to be some sort of superhero - an alien, perhaps. But her freckle-laden face, ruddy cheeks, flaming red hair and light blue eyes suggested a heritage more Celtic than extraterrestrial.

The poster on the left emits the text of what is clearly intended to be an advertisement for whatever is going on. It's simple and to the point...

CHILDREN!!!!!!
For One Day Only- TODAY!!!!
CAPTAIN FANTASTIC
THE FASTEST, STRONGEST
AND

...explains EXACTLY how she obtained her mighty powers and how *you* can get *your* greatest wishes *achieved.*

Today- Courtyard- 2 PM
NO ADULTS PERMITTED!!!!!

Well, I thought. *That's kind of strange. It must be rather important to be kept a secret.* But what it didn't say was that I couldn't try to talk to her about it afterwards.

***

I waited until about 3 PM, at which point the demonstration/lecture ended and the young patrons streamed out *en masse*. Somehow, I managed to get towards the Captain herself, still on the dais erected outside for her, wearing the uniform she wore in the poster along with some black riding boots. She saw me and frowned.

"What do you want?" she asked. "I said 'no adults' here for a very good reason."

"I'm a reporter," I responded. "I just want a little of your time for an interview."

Her frown shifted into a beaming smile.

"Well!" she said. "It's about time one of you types took me seriously." She pursed her lips. "The kids get me completely, especially the really young ones. But, when I try to tell adults about my story, they just *laugh*. Can you *imagine*?" She threw her hands up in frustration. "More than once, I nearly lost it and committed murder with my fists. Some superhero behavior that is, huh?"

She walked down off the stage towards me.

"Come on. I need to find a place to take off. Too crowded here, and I might hurt somebody. Don't worry - I won't run. You can keep up with me that way."

I agreed to this, and retrieved my pen and paper, taking down what she told me in bullet points.

***

"First of all, Captain Fantastic isn't my real name - obviously. My real one is Olivia. Olivia Thrift, and....DAMN IT! I TOLD somebody! You better NOT tell *anybody* about this, or I'LL....DO...*SOMETHING* to you!"

I assured her that my profession required me to keep such information private, and she had nothing to fear from confiding in me. That reassured her.

"Okay," she continued, putting a finger to her brain. "Now, where was I?.....Ah, yeah.

"I come from a small town in Manitoba, and I didn't have a lot of friends. I mean, really close ones. Other than my best friend, Dixon Wells, who's the only guy who really knows who I am, but that's about it. So, what with my parents working in Winnipeg most of the time, and Dixon not always being around to play with, I was kind of left alone with the television. I know: total latchkey kid, right? But you grow up faster that way - I know *that*.

"I've always been a fan of cartoons, 'specially the superhero ones. And I always wanted to be one of them. You understand?" I nodded. "Well, one night while I was in the midst of watching something on the set concentrating, you see, not just gazing at it a spirit materialized in front of me. Somehow or other it knew my name. I was dressed like this save for the boots, found them at the Sally Ann. And the spirit said: *You desire becoming a superhero so you can save the world.* And I said, 'Yeah!' Then he said: *Do you wish to be the fastest, strongest and smartest one of your kind on Earth?* I said, 'Yeah!' And then he said: *Then it shall be done.* And I got zapped by him. Like a whole electrical power station through me! And then I became like I am now. No fooling."

She stopped and looked up at me.

"This is normally where the adults start laughing. But you aren't."

"Well, I specialize in writing about children with….special abilities….so I can take you as seriously as you want me to," I explained.

"So you write comics? Sorry: I mean *graphic novels*?"

"No. Prose fiction."

"And *that* is?"

"Short stories. Novels."

"Ah. Got it. *Any*-way….

"I tried my best to be secretive about it at first, and I could do it with everybody, except Dixon. He's even smarter than I am, that guy. He saw me wrecking an out-of-tune piano one day when I thought no one was looking, and I threatened him by saying I'd do the same thing to HIM if he spilled it. That's how we teamed up. He convinced me that a girl with my abilities *had* to go out and save the world and stuff, 'cause it would be a big loss to the world if I didn't. And so I went out and started doing it, and then, after I'd save the world a couple of times, people wanted me to tell them about how I got so strong and fast and junk. I wasn't sure what to do, so I tried to contact the spirit who had "gifted me" with my mind powers. I found him and told him about it.

"He told me that any child who hasn't reached physical maturity can reach him and his kind telepathically if they know how to do it. Which he told me. This can only be done if you're watching TV and staring into it right up straight, the way I was, as you turn the set on and tune in. Hence, "Tune-Ism."

"I decided that I was going to spread the word about this. We kids have very little power in this world, as you know, and I thought this was a good way to create some. Dixon wasn't too happy about it at first, but he came around soon enough after I...uh...."persuaded" him that it was a good idea. So, in between battling evil, I help kids understand how to channel their inner mental abilities to get what they want.

"Of course, in doing so, I ended up creating two big problems for myself. Two other kids who attended some of my seminars and figured out how to connect the way I did. They got what they wanted, and boy, did it mean trouble for me.

"First was Gridiron Girl, a tomboy who wanted to be the toughest and sportiest girl on Earth, and got granted the power of a full football team after that. I tried to stop her but she was even stronger than me. One punch from her literally knocked me out of my uniform! Not only that, but she was fast enough to keep up with me in a footrace. That's where having the smarts comes in handy, 'cause she didn't have any. Athletes, you know? So I grabbed a goal post, tied it around her, and kicked her to the other side of the world. Hopefully, she won't be back.

"Then there's the Jester. He's into 'toons like I am, 'cept he prefers the ones that were done for laughs a long time ago. So he plays for laughs, too, only they aren't funny. Pranks and hotfoots and cream pies in the face and tricking me into running off cliffs and falling down. That sort of thing. I finally decided that if you couldn't beat him, you had to join 'em. So that's what Dixon and I did...."

She would probably have continued in this vein, but a phone rang. Hers. She fished it out of her pocket and answered it.

"Hello. Yeah, Dixon....WHAT? How did she....I fixed it so that she could never....UUHHH! Those *villains*! I'll be right there, kid. Don't worry."

She turned to me.

"Sorry, fella. I gotta go." She shook my hand carefully to avoid breaking it with her strength, and prepared to fly off into the sky. "Just make sure that you don't give away any of my secrets, okay? FAREWELL!!!!!"

Now, you might expect that she was not able to fly along with her other "mighty" powers, and that her brash manner was simply a way of covering up the fact that she really did not possess these powers, and that the whole idea of Tune-Ism was simply a product of her overactive, pre-adolescent mind.

You would be wrong.

Belong Together
By
Ed Cooke

Hilary hated job interviews. They were the sort of elaborate trap best reserved for particularly rare and cunning animals.

He sat and sweated into the collar that had been a perfect fit the previous summer. None of the three people on the other side of the table gave him anything to go on. Which was ridiculous: the point of the exercise was to get to know each other a little, just enough to determine whether Hilary would be a good fit for the role.

Of course the role had nothing to do with it. The goal was to see whether Hilary would be a good fit for the other people.

The interviewer in the middle sighed. The one on his left twiddled her pencil and he one on his right had abandoned all pretence of attention and was candy crushing openly. These were not good signs. Millennia of practice told Hilary these were not good signs.

"Why did you leave your previous job?"

That was an extremely bad sign.

Hilary was not even sure which interviewer had spoken. It hardly mattered. None of this would: not in a hundred years, not after lunch.

Hilary took a deep breath. He breathed from his diaphragm, the way his acting teacher had instructed him, back in the days when he could still afford drama classes.

"It's because of my disability."

That word got a momentary glance up from the iPhone, a slowing of the pencil's ceaseless rotation. Nothing more. This was going to be a hard sell. It always was.

"It's called "communitism." Nothing to do with Marx. Nor Engels."

"I haven't heard of that," the lady said guardedly.

"You wouldn't have. You probably don't suffer from it yourself."'

Too much too soon. The lady put down her pencil, aligning it millimetrically with the edge of her notebook. Nobody liked their own insensitivity revealed to them, as Hilary well knew. He would have to take a different tack, and quickly.

"What it is, I have this deep-seated need to be part of a community."

"Don't we all?" Without looking up from the iPhone.

"We do. I mean, of course. It goes way back. Evolutionary psychology and so forth. But with me it's serious."

The middle man said, "All the people who've ever sat in that chair tell us they're team players. They contribute something. They change the outcome of projects. They directly affect deliverables. And not one of them ever thought of that as a disability. I might be forgiven for suspecting they made it up because they thought it would impress us."

"I understand that, sir, but people like that... They're just as bad as people who say they're depressed, when all they mean is they're very sad."

"I don't see the connection."

"I really want to be around other people."

"Really? Most of us just want to be alone."

"I realise that. But that's because you've never seriously thought about how many other people your solitude depends on. You're never alone: not as long as there are clothes on your back and food in your belly.

"For me, and others like me, the very idea is intolerable. No man is in himself an island, and so forth. Nor," he added hastily, "is any woman. That's the essence of communitism.

"The trouble with my last job was that I didn't experience enough human contact. You can tell a great deal about people by inspecting the contents of their dustbin, but it's no substitute for the contact I crave. Because of my condition."

The middle interviewer said, "Well, it goes without saying that we'll take that into consideration."

The lady looked at the clock and said, "Well, we are running late and we have several other candidates to see."

The man with the iPhone set it down on the table. "I have a question."

Both his colleagues shot him warning glances obvious to Hilary. The man blithely ignored them.

"Ask yourself this: do you really want to work here?"

Panic hurtled across his colleagues' faces. Hilary hoped none was to be seen on his own. *What kind of hard man was this? Did he think this was any way to treat someone with a disability?*

"Think about it, think hard about whether this is the right place for you."

"Well of course I have and it's--"

The interviewer silenced Hilary with the mildest of frowns. "Is it? Is it now?"

Feral silence roamed the room. The man in the middle obviously had the lion's share of responsibility for delivering the outcome of a new employee. Hilary thought he had given this fellow what he needed: a swift solution that bolstered his self-image as an equal opportunities employer. Was he going to let himself be overruled by a lippy subordinate?

"If we set you on here," iPhone Man said, "we will be putting you in a cubicle and providing the barest semblance of contact with your fellows. You will be expected to work alongside people with whom you have nothing in common and for whom not even a self-confessed communitist could give a fig. You will be in constant touch by telephone with people whom you will be expected to manipulate to meet or exceed our business goals.

"It seems to me that the sort of person we are looking for, for this particular role, is someone who does not suffer from your unfortunate condition. In fact, a mild sociopath would be ideal. We're prepared to overlook all the usual guff about being a team player because we doubt anybody really means it, but we simply wouldn't have the resources to provide you the specialist support you need.

'We do sympathize with your different ability, and as a gesture of goodwill we would be happy to make a donation to any charity that tries to serve your needs."

He sat back and folded his arms.

Hilary got to his feet. He did this smoothly, without tremor. He shook all three hands, moving right to left, ladies first, and grinned his biggest grin, clamping three successive paws inside both of his. This part he was far too familiar with, this part he had never even imagined existed because no-one ever spoke of repeated failure. Even though that was how Nature worked.

Very likely he was genuinely suffering from failurism, but that wouldn't land him a job. He might mention it to Louise, later, in bed, once she'd finished bawling him out for blowing yet another interview. Not as badly, he would argue, as the time he tried to persuade the bus company he would need special treatment on account of his allergy to all the colours in their livery. Or the graduate training for management accountancy, where they had not appeared remotely interested in his chronic Pythagorism.

Communitism had been his own invention. It was Louise's turn next time to think of something that would give him an edge.

Under Pressure
By
Katherine Park

High school sucks. It is portrayed as fun and games, but not for me.

I was a part of the varsity cheer squad, in honors classes, and had the hottest boyfriend in my grade. This mattered a great deal to me, and the only way I could keep these things was to subject my mind, body and soul to great torture. I would skip meals and pressure my body into more pain by enduring two, hour long cheer practices every school day and late night study sessions with my boyfriend that almost always led to things she didn't want to do. But that's all a part of being a teenage girl nowadays. I often defined my days as the epitome of "pressurism."

Pressured by the cheer captains to stay a certain weight, I eventually became bulimic to please them. I stayed on the captains' good sides and did everything they said, just the way they said it. Ashley and Emma, the current cheer captains, terrified me. They ruled the school. People feared them. When they would walk into a room, people would move out of the way.

Of the two, Emma was the most approachable but could often turn against you and hurt your reputation in a millisecond. During Emma's freshmen year, she was sitting with a group of people and a girl named Harriet misspoke and corrected Emma about something. This put Emma in a frenzy and caused her to tweet out a hideous tweet about

Harriet. This one tweet caused Harriet to spiral from the top of the social hierarchy all the way to the bottom. Emma was even able to convince some of Harriet's closest friends to turn against her and leave her behind. Luckily for most of the girls on the squad, Emma liked them and didn't do this sort of stuff to them.

Captain Ashley was the captain that everyone feared most and she had no good side to her. On the outside, she looked like the sweetest girl on the planet with beautiful hair and perfect skin. But once you begin to talk to her, you notice just how judgmental and rude she is. Without even knowing me, Ashley began to talk about me, loudly, behind my back. She commented on my thin stringy hair saying she wouldn't survive living with hair like that.

Unfortunately for me, I did not look like the typical small, blond and cute varsity cheer girl. Instead, I was a tall, gangly brunette and my face, unfortunately, always seemed to have a scowl. The pressure of looking perfect definitely hit me hard and caused me to become extremely sensitive to people around me and to anything people said to me.

"Come on girls, let's get it together and start practice. FIVE. SIX. SEVEN. EIGHT!" screamed lead captain Ashley at practice one night.

Instantly my mind spun and I felt the pressure of Ashley's eyes fall on her. The girls fell in line to Ashley's commands and began to lift people in the air. Multiple times Ashley screamed at them to hit their stunts. They had to be perfect and could not fall apart. Well into practice, I finally had enough. The stunts failed time and time again before Emma suggested the team take a water break.

Collapsing from exhaustion, I finally got a break from the torture of practice and went over to grab some water. The girls and I rubbed our sore muscles and sipped water from our bottles. They were as done with the practice as I was.

I, unfortunately, had a tough spot in the stunt section. I was in charge of catching the middle flyer, the most important flyer.

"Let's hit it one last time, girls," yelled Ashley. "We have to hit this perfect right now."

I rolled my eyes and lugged my body back to my position. I couldn't wait to get out of practice and go home and relax.

Thirty minutes and a few bruises later, Emma called the practice and let the girls go. Before letting them go, she asked me to stay back and speak to her and Ashley.

"Listen, Lily, we need you to step it up at practices. You don't realize just how much pressure we are under. We have to get this routine to look top notch and frankly, your attitude is not helping."

"Excuse me, but I catch my girl and I do not let her drop. I do my job, I do it well, and I enjoy doing it. Yes, sometimes I'm ready to leave early, but when told to do my job, I hit it and I hit it hard. I crush this routine."

Taken aback, I couldn't help but laugh.

"Excuse me, missy, but are you the captain here?" snapped Ashley. "If we tell you to do something differently, you better."

"Ashley, calm down," suggested Emma, "This isn't how things should be fixed. We should talk civilly."

While they fought back and forth, I could not wait to get home and to let loose. I was planning on getting high that night. Things had been difficult at home and school and I needed to get rid of the extra pressure. This was my only way to escape the reality of life. I received pressure from my parents, my teachers, my coaches, my friends, and from my own mind. By getting high, I was able to escape all of these pressures and could relax comfortably in my own world.

"How much longer do y'all need me?" I asked. "I have to go home and start homework."

"I guess if you're not as committed as we thought," said Ashley. "You can go now I suppose."

Practically running off, I set off for my car to head home. I was ready to enter my own happy world. I would gather food around me and turn on my favorite show, *New Girl*, and watch and eat food all night. At some point, I would have to make myself get sick so I wouldn't gain any weight, but I enjoyed the food while I ate.

As I watched the show, I smoked a joint and gradually felt myself drift away. I was finally pressure free.

About the writers:

J. J. Steinfeld lives on Prince Edward Island, where he is patiently waiting for Godot's arrival. While waiting, he has published sixteen books, including *Disturbing Identities* (Stories, Ekstasis Editions), *Should the Word Hell Be Capitalized?* (Stories, Gaspereau Press), *Would You Hide Me?* (Stories, Gaspereau Press), *Misshapenness* (Poetry, Ekstasis Editions), *Identity Dreams and Memory Sounds* +(Poetry, Ekstasis Editions), and *Madhouses in Heaven, Castles in Hell* (Stories, Ekstasis Editions).

Matthew J. Hall is a UK writer based in Bristol. His Poetry chapbook, Pigeons and Peace Doves is available through Blood Pudding Press. Hear more from him at www.screamingwithbrevity.com where he highlights and reviews new writing within the small press.

After years of considering himself a writer, **Paul Rhodes** decided that it was time to stop scribbling on beer mats and cocktail napkins and get serious. His short story "Blind Man's Bluff" appeared in the FTB Press anthology, "Irrational Fears." He lives in Faversham, England, with his wife, Faye, and son, Dylan.

Diane Arrelle, the pen name of **Dina Leacock**, has sold more than 200 short stories and has two published books. Recently retired from being director of a municipal senior citizen center, she lives with her husband and her cat on the edge of the Pine Barrens in Southern New Jersey (home of the Jersey Devil).

Essel Pratt is the author of Final Reverie and ABC's of Zombie Friendship. His writings have appeared in over 40 publications, ranging across multiple genres, although focusing mostly on horror. He is the Co-Host of the Wicked Little Things podcast on Blog Talk Radio and is also the Event Calendar Coordinator for the Horror Writers Association.

Edward Ahern resumed writing after forty odd years in foreign intelligence and international sales. Over ninety stories and poems published so far, and two books. Original wife, but after forty eight years we are both out of warranty.

Lance Hyden was born in the mean no, high-spirited streets of Detroit, Michigan. He traded the cold for heat by moving to Phoenix, Arizona during high school. After being stationed in California while serving in the Marine Corp, Lance moved back to Michigan and graduated from Eastern Michigan University with a degree in film. Finding the sun more attractive than the snow, Lance moved back to Arizona where he lives with his girlfriend and their 4 boys.

Sarah Doebereiner is a short story author, novelist, and poet. She graduated from Wright State University in 2010 with her BA in English. Sarah lives in central Ohio with her husband and two small children. Macabre themes fascinate her because of their tendency to stay with readers long after the book has closed.

Tracey Chapman has two sons and work as a taxi driver and painter and decorator. His last work was published with FTB Press and working towards new projects.

Charly Douglas, with an array of life experiences from riding in the 'hell hole' of a Huey to wandering the back streets of foreign cities, draws inspirations from experiences in the fields of Intelligence, Linguistics, Science and Analytics.

DJ Tyrer is the person behind *Atlantean Publishing* and has been published in *Irrational Fears* (FTB Press) *State of Horror: Illinois* (Charon Coin Press), *Strangely Funny II* (Mystery & Horror LLC), *Destroy All Robots* (Dynatox Ministries), and *Ill-considered Expeditions* (April Moon Books), and in addition, has a novella available ithrough Amazon, *The Yellow House* (Dunhams Manor).

Karen Robiscoe's work has appeared in literary journals: Spectrum at UCSB, Postscripts to Darkness, KY Story, Bohemia Journal, Steamticket Journal, Peachfuzz Magazine, Dark Light 3, Bibliotheca Alexandrina, Main Street Rag, Meat for Tea, Sand Canyon Review, & Midnight Circus, and Peachfish. Fowlpox Press released her chapbook: Word Mosaics in 2014.

Veronica Smith lives in Katy, Texas, west of Houston. She has written many short stories, and started several books but only recently beeb published. Veronica currently has 3 short stories in publication and several others in the process of being published.
www.facebook.com/Veronica.Smith.Author

Matt McGee writes short fiction in the library because it's free. He sits in local fast food restaurants, not eating but using their Wi-Fi all the same. He has never driven a GT40 but is contemplating a career in the parking arts with hopes that a chance will come his way. His short story 'Unseen Among Kings' was nominated for the 2015 Pushcart Award and his collection 'Leaving Rayette' is available on Amazon.

Samuel Kim is an emerging writer from Fort Worth, Texas. His favorite genres are action and romance. He loves eating breakfast food, reading/writing/blogging, sleeping, spending time with friends and family, and exploring downtown and the wilderness

Matthew Aufiero is an emerging writer of sci-fi short stories and plays. His true love in writing is novels and poetry which he is still working on completing. When he is not writing, he is reading science fiction or watching South Park and the Daily Show.

Anne Wilson's short fiction appears in various anthologies. Recently *'Swapping Beads'* was selected for *The Momaya*

Short Story Review 2015. Her first novel is a murder mystery, *Here Be Dragons: A Tale of Mortals, Myths and Mystery*, set in Mallorca and in Denmark. www.anne@authoranne.co.uk

Catherine A. MacKenzie writes poems and short fiction women relate to. She's been published in print and online publications. She has self-published short story collections, poetry books, and children's picture books. Cathy lives in Halifax, Nova Scotia, and winters in Ajijic, Mexico, where her works have appeared in publications. www.writingwicket.wordpress.com

Glen Damien Campbell lives and works in London. His horror fiction has appeared in a variety of anthologies and magazines, including Something Wicked Vol. One, 100 Doors to Madness, Tales of the Undead: Suffer Eternal, Tales from the Blue Gonk Café and Miseria's Chorale. Besides writing, his interests are music, painting and horror movies. For more information about Glen, or to read his jottings on various things horror related, visit his blog at gdcampbell.wordpress.com.

Mary Steer currently leads a less extraordinary life than many of her characters, but this doesn't stop her from dreaming. In the past she has indulged in her fair share of oddisms and plans to write about them all.

David Perlmutter is a freelance writer based in Winnipeg, Manitoba, Canada. The holder of an MA degree from the Universities of Manitoba and Winnipeg, and a lifelong animation fan, he has published short fiction in a variety of genres for various magazines and anthologies, as well as essays on his favorite topics for similar publishers. He is the author of *America Toons In: A History of Television Animation* (McFarland and Co.), *The Singular Adventures Of Jefferson Ball* (Chupa Cabra House), *The Pups* (Booklocker.com), *Certain Private Conversations and Other Stories* (Aurora Publishing), *Orthicon; or, the History of a Bad Idea (*Linkville Press, forthcoming) and *Nothing About Us Without Us: The Adventures of the Cartoon Republican Army* (Dreaming Big Productions, forthcoming.)

Ed Cooke is a freelance technical writer and translator based in York, UK. He has been published by Stairwell Books, Pink Narcissus Press and Timeless Tales Magazine. Cooke has also written half-a-dozen stage musicals and one short film.

Katherine Park, a young author, writes short stories in the genres of young adult and romance. When not writing short stories, Katherine enjoys reading books, hanging with family and friends, trying out new restaurants and watching movies.